FOR THE LOVE OF SCOTLAND

"Are you really sending me away – for ever?" Julia stammered. "And just where do you suggest that I should – go?"

Despite her effort to speak quietly and sound brave, her voice trembled on the last word.

"What I am suggesting," her stepmother said, "will certainly be to your advantage. It will give you what I feel every woman really wants and indeed craves for and that is a home of her own."

Julia looked puzzled.

She did not understand.

Then her stepmother said almost harshly as if she was thinking that Julia was being rather stupid,

"I am proposing to you that you should be married and your father agrees with me that no one could be more suitable than one of our neighbours."

Julia gave a little gasp.

THE BARBARA CARTLAND PINK COLLECTION

Titles in this series

1. The Cross Of Love
2. Love In The Highlands
3. Love Finds The Way
4. The Castle Of Love
5. Love Is Triumphant
6. Stars In The Sky
7. The Ship Of Love
8. A Dangerous Disguise
9. Love Became Theirs
10. Love Drives In
11. Sailing To Love
12. The Star Of Love
13. Music Is The Soul Of Love
14. Love In The East
15. Theirs To Eternity
16. A Paradise On Earth
17. Love Wins In Berlin
18. In Search Of Love
19. Love Rescues Rosanna
20. A Heart In Heaven
21. The House Of Happiness
22. Royalty Defeated By Love
23. The White Witch
24. They Sought Love
25. Love Is The Reason For Living
26. They Found Their Way To Heaven
27. Learning To Love
28. Journey To Happiness
29. A Kiss In The Desert
30. The Heart Of Love
31. The Richness Of Love
32. For Ever And Ever
33. An Unexpected Love
34. Saved By An Angel
35. Touching The Stars
36. Seeking Love
37. Journey To Love
38. The Importance Of Love
39. Love By The Lake
40. A Dream Come True
41. The King Without A Heart
42. The Waters Of Love
43. Danger To The Duke
44. A Perfect Way To Heaven
45. Follow Your Heart
46. In Hiding
47. Rivals For Love
48. A Kiss From The Heart
49. Lovers In London
50. This Way To Heaven
51. A Princess Prays
52. Mine For Ever
53. The Earl's Revenge
54. Love At The Tower
55. Ruled By Love
56. Love Came From Heaven
57. Love And Apollo
58. The Keys Of Love
59. A Castle Of Dreams
60. A Battle Of Brains
61. A Change Of Hearts
62. It Is Love
63. The Triumph Of Love
64. Wanted – A Royal Wife
65. A Kiss Of Love
66. To Heaven With Love
67. Pray For Love
68. The Marquis Is Trapped
69. Hide And Seek For Love
70. Hiding From Love
71. A Teacher Of Love
72. Money Or Love
73. The Revelation Is Love
74. The Tree Of Love
75. The Magnificent Marquis
76. The Castle
77. The Gates Of Paradise
78. A Lucky Star
79. A Heaven On Earth
80. The Healing Hand
81. A Virgin Bride
82. The Trail To Love
83. A Royal Love Match
84. A Steeplechase For Love
85. Love At Last
86. Search For A Wife
87. Secret Love
88. A Miracle Of Love
89. Love And The Clans
90. A Shooting Star
91. The Winning Post Is Love
92. They Touched Heaven
93. The Mountain Of Love
94. The Queen Wins
95. Love And The Gods
96. Joined By Love
97. The Duke Is Deceived
98. A Prayer For Love
99. Love Conquers War
100. A Rose In Jeopardy
101. A Call Of Love
102. A Flight To Heaven
103. She Wanted Love
104. A Heart Finds Love
105. A Sacrifice For Love
106. Love's Dream In Peril
107. Soft, Sweet And Gentle
108. An Archangel Called Ivan
109. A Prisoner In Paris
110. Danger In The Desert
111. Rescued By Love
112. A Road To Romance
113. A Golden Lie
114. A Heart Of Stone
115. The Earl Elopes
116. A Wilder Kind Of Love
117. The Bride Runs Away
118. Beyond The Horizon
119. Crowned By Music
120. Love Solves The Problem
121. Blessing Of The Gods
122. Love By Moonlight
123. Saved By The Duke
124. A Train To Love
125. Wanted – A Bride
126. Double The Love
127. Hiding From The Fortune-Hunters
128. The Marquis Is Deceived
129. The Viscount's Revenge
130. Captured By Love
131. An Ocean Of Love
132. A Beauty Betrayed
133. No Bride, No Wedding
134. A Strange Way To Find Love
135. The Unbroken Dream
136. A Heart In Chains
137. One Minute To Love
138. Love For Eternity
139. The Prince Who Wanted Love
140. For The Love Of Scotland

FOR THE LOVE OF SCOTLAND

BARBARA CARTLAND

Barbaracartland.com Ltd

THE BARBARA CARTLAND PINK COLLECTION

Dame Barbara Cartland is still regarded as the most prolific bestselling author in the history of the world.

In her lifetime she was frequently in the Guinness Book of Records for writing more books than any other living author.

Her most amazing literary feat was to double her output from 10 books a year to over 20 books a year when she was 77 to meet the huge demand.

She went on writing continuously at this rate for 20 years and wrote her very last book at the age of 97, thus completing an incredible 400 books between the ages of 77 and 97.

Her publishers finally could not keep up with this phenomenal output, so at her death in 2000 she left behind an amazing 160 unpublished manuscripts, something that no other author has ever achieved.

Barbara's son, Ian McCorquodale, together with his daughter Iona, felt that it was their sacred duty to publish all these titles for Barbara's millions of admirers all over the world who so love her wonderful romances.

So in 2004 they started publishing the 160 brand new Barbara Cartlands as *The Barbara Cartland Pink Collection*, as Barbara's favourite colour was always pink – and yet more pink!

The Barbara Cartland Pink Collection is published monthly exclusively by Barbaracartland.com and the books are numbered in sequence from 1 to 160.

Enjoy receiving a brand new Barbara Cartland book each month by taking out an annual subscription to the Pink Collection, or purchase the books individually.

The Pink Collection is available from the Barbara Cartland website www.barbaracartland.com via mail order and through all good bookshops.

In addition Ian and Iona are proud to announce that The Barbara Cartland Pink Collection is now available in ebook format as from Valentine's Day 2011.

For more information, please contact us at:

Barbaracartland.com Ltd.
Camfield Place
Hatfield
Hertfordshire AL9 6JE
United Kingdom

Telephone: +44 (0)1707 642629
Fax: +44 (0)1707 663041
Email: info@barbaracartland.com

THE LATE DAME BARBARA CARTLAND

Barbara Cartland who sadly died in May 2000 at the age of nearly 99 was the world's most famous romantic novelist who wrote 723 books in her lifetime with worldwide sales of over 1 billion copies and her books were translated into 36 different languages.

As well as romantic novels, she wrote historical biographies, 6 autobiographies, theatrical plays, books of advice on life, love, vitamins and cookery. She also found time to be a political speaker and television and radio personality.

She wrote her first book at the age of 21 and this was called *Jigsaw*. It became an immediate bestseller and sold 100,000 copies in hardback and was translated into 6 different languages. She wrote continuously throughout her life, writing bestsellers for an astonishing 76 years. Her books have always been immensely popular in the United States, where in 1976 her current books were at numbers 1 & 2 in the B. Dalton bestsellers list, a feat never achieved before or since by any author.

Barbara Cartland became a legend in her own lifetime and will be best remembered for her wonderful romantic novels, so loved by her millions of readers throughout the world.

Her books will always be treasured for their moral message, her pure and innocent heroines, her good looking and dashing heroes and above all her belief that the power of love is more important than anything else in everyone's life.

"I am proud of my Scottish blood and, when I cross the border from England into Scotland, there is always a tremor of excitement running through my veins. And, who knows, there could be a hint of romance in those brooding hills and in the deep purple of the heather."

Barbara Cartland

CHAPTER ONE
1868

Julia climbed out of bed and then pulled back the curtains from her bedroom window.

It was wide open and at once the sun enveloped her in its rays.

She realised, as she expected, that it was a beautiful day and it would be very hot later on.

She glanced down at the garden which seemed to her to become more beautiful every day and certainly every summer.

Even as a small child she had been delighted when her Nanny had pushed her pram into the flower garden.

She would delight at the continual buzzing of the bees circling round the flowers and the butterflies fluttering above them.

She knew when she looked out now that she must go into the garden as soon as possible.

Hurriedly she then pulled on her clothes taking out the first dress that came to hand from the wardrobe.

She thought that it was not herself who would look attractive, but the flowers she was longing to see as well as swathes of spring blossom.

It only took her just a few minutes to dress and she brushed her hair without even looking in the mirror to see if it was tidy and neat.

Then she ran to the door and pulled it open.

It was so early in the morning that the servants had not yet drawn the curtains. The passage was in darkness with only a faint glimmer of light emanating from the hall below.

There was, however, no need for guidance.

She was only too anxious to be in the garden and to be surrounded by beauty.

She had lived at The Manor since she was born and to her it was the most beautiful house in the world without any exceptions.

She ran down the stairs, unlocked the door and let herself out.

Then, as the sunshine covered her, she ran into the flower garden.

She felt that the flowers were waiting for her and they needed her as much as she needed them.

*

It was three hours later that Julia went back to her bedroom to tidy herself for breakfast.

She had spent all those hours, as she so loved to do, amongst the glorious kaleidoscope of flowers.

She had walked down from the garden towards the lake.

She wanted to swim in the cool water, but she had promised her father that, as the lake was so old and deep, she would never swim there alone.

She would always have someone watching her just in case she got into trouble. It was a promise that she had always kept, because the lake was so much an integral part of her life.

Just as the garden and house were the background to everything she thought about and felt in her heart and soul.

Now the front door was open and the servants had already brushed and dusted the hall.

She went slowly up the stairs looking with pleasure at the magnificent pictures above the mantelpiece and on the walls on either side of it.

A great number of the pictures had been collected by her father's family all down the centuries.

They were the great pride and delight of the family including Julia's older brother, who would one day inherit them when he succeeded to her father's title.

What her father had said and what she knew always lay at the back of his mind was that he himself was the only member of their illustrious family who had not been able to add to its marvellous collection.

Because life had altered so much over the centuries, the Westwoods were not as rich as they had been more than a hundred years ago.

In fact they now had to spend their money with the greatest care.

They most certainly could not add to the pictures or to the library as her father's ancestors had managed to do so successfully.

In fact the library was often quoted as being one of the finest privately owned libraries in the country.

Just as his pictures were spoken of and admired all over the world.

'If we had more money,' Julia thought, 'we could buy more horses.'

She forced herself to be content with the fact that the horses in the stables were excellent, but there was not the number she would have liked to have filled the empty stalls.

However, because she loved her home so sincerely, she forced herself not to criticise when a picture needed restoring or a book was for sale that should have added to their collection, but which they certainly could not afford now.

Although she well realised that her father longed to purchase them, he was forced not to bid for them for the simple reason that he could not afford it.

As she reached the top of the stairs, she then heard someone moving about below.

Glancing down she saw her stepmother coming out of the dining room where she had obviously just finished breakfast.

With a start Julia realised that, because she had so enjoyed being in the garden and down by the lake, it was far later than she had thought.

Her stepmother would have finished breakfast and would be extremely annoyed that she had not been present for the meal.

Hurriedly she went to her bedroom in order to tidy herself before she ran down the stairs.

Her stepmother heard her coming and turned round.

"Oh, so there you are, Julia," she said sharply. "I suppose you realise that you are late as usual for breakfast and have just wasted your time, as you usually do, messing about in the garden, when you should have had breakfast with me."

"I am sorry, Stepmama," Julia replied, "but it was such a lovely morning and the sun was shining on the lake. I saw a large number of baby ducklings that were not there yesterday. It was so exciting to see them swimming behind their proud mother."

She then realised, as she finished speaking, that her stepmother was not going to answer.

She was merely frowning, as she usually did when she came into contact with her stepdaughter.

Julia had no illusions.

She well knew that her stepmother disliked her.

She had done so since she had come to the house thrilled and delighted at being the bride of the sixth Earl of Westwood.

They had met in France where she was, at the time, living with one of her relatives as her parents were both dead.

Mildred Fernway had been totally thrilled at having outwitted all her pushing contemporaries by making such a brilliant marriage.

She had not anticipated or even thought about the fact that he had children by his previous wife.

The Earl had been extremely happy with the girl he had married when she was very young.

She had given him two sons and a daughter besides being, in every way, exactly what one could have expected of a Countess.

She was adored by all the people on the estate and by those in the villages owned by her husband and there were quite a number of them.

The only blot on their complete happiness during their marriage was the fact that the Earl found it more and more difficult to keep the house and his large estate in the perfection he always desired for them.

Expenses grew greater and greater every year and the money which he had inherited from his ancestors grew smaller.

In fact, when the boys were old enough to go to Eton where their father had been educated, the Earl had found it difficult to pay for their fees.

Also to give a big 'coming out' ball, which he fully knew was anticipated of him, for his daughter.

Somehow he and his wife had really struggled to give her the balls that were expected in the country and in London.

They knew that the whole of their family would be horrified if what had taken place all down the centuries was ignored and Julia had to be content with a luncheon party or perhaps a tea-party down by the lake with just a few of her contemporaries.

Although it was impossible for the Earl to sell any of the treasures that ornamented the walls of The Manor, because like everything else they were all entailed onto his eldest son, although he did in fact sell a necklace which his grandmother had contributed to the family jewels.

He hoped fervently that no one would realise that it was missing.

Julia, therefore, was able to be given her official coming out ball in London.

It was not held in the house in Park Lane which had been let for ten years to someone who could afford the very considerable expenses it entailed, but in the house of one of her father's aunts.

She had been fortunate to marry a rich man and this was accepted without much comment.

But the huge ball in the country which everyone of importance in the County expected to be invited to, was an occasion that could not take place anywhere else but in the ballroom of The Manor.

It was large and, as it had not been used for some years, it required a great deal of hard work before it was useable.

But the ball had certainly been an unprecedented success.

Julia had been acclaimed by all those present as the most beautiful *debutante* besides being the most successful one of the year.

It was shortly after this that the Countess, who had never been especially strong since her second son had been born, died unexpectedly.

It was an undeniable shock to her family, especially her husband.

He had been extremely happy with his wife and he had often thought that he was the luckiest man in the world because he had a wife he loved and who loved him.

He also had an heir to his ancient title, which he was inordinately proud of.

He owned a Manor House filled with treasures that made everyone who looked at them exclaim how fortunate he was in a way which told him clearly that they envied him for being the possessor of so much wealth.

What they did not know, he thought bitterly, was that it was difficult to give his treasures the background to which they were entitled.

There were parts of The Manor that were very old and long overdue for repair.

The staff attending to the house and family had to be reduced year by year simply because he could not afford their wages.

The garden that gave Julia such happiness was very spectacular where it could be seen, but sadly it was in need of attention in so many other parts, which fortunately were hidden from visitors.

Only Julia knew just how difficult it was for the few gardeners they could afford to keep such a large area from running completely wild.

She admitted to herself that the kitchen garden was a disgrace except for a small portion of it which provided the fresh vegetables needed by the family.

But, because she loved it just as it was and would never criticise it even to herself, she refused to face the fact that a great part of the family assets were falling into rack and ruin.

But she was content because it was her home which she loved.

It was two years after her mother's death that her father was invited to France.

As the good friend who invited him was paying all his expenses because they were to be travelling together, he accepted the invitation.

He not only wanted to visit France but his doctors informed him that he needed a change of air and they had no wish to have him as an ill patient.

He had to admit to himself that he enjoyed being with his friends and being abroad.

What no one expected, especially his family, was that he would marry again and return home with his new bride.

'Just how could he possibly want to marry anyone,' Julia had asked herself, 'when he was so happy with Mama and so utterly miserable when she died?'

It was a question which was answered when she met the bride.

She was the one daughter of a distinguished French Nobleman and her mother had been an American. She had inherited very much more from her mother than from her father.

In fact it was difficult for anyone to think that she was anything but an American.

She was attractive and was always very generous with her money.

That she was in love with the Earl was obvious.

But Julia realised that from the moment she arrived, she resented his daughter and to a certain extent his sons.

However, because her father seemed to be in better health and happier than when he had left England, Julia forced herself to accept the fact that she had a stepmother, who she knew instinctively disliked and resented her from the moment that they were first introduced.

As she was so thrilled at becoming a Countess and at the same time genuinely in love with the Earl himself, Mildred had thought that she was being swept away into a Heaven on earth.

Her future life would be exactly as she had always planned and schemed it should be.

What she had not anticipated and was only aware of it when she arrived in England was that the Earl's eldest child was grown up.

Besides that, Julia was exceedingly beautiful, which somehow made her own beauty fade considerably.

She had known, of course, that the Earl had three children. But because the two boys were at school, she had expected the girl to be about the same age or even younger than the boys.

But no one in France had bothered to tell her that Julia had already been acclaimed as the *debutante* of the year in London.

She was undoubtedly beautiful in a very different way from the new Countess.

Mildred's face was very American in some ways, except that her large dark eyes which spoke for themselves were undoubtedly French.

Her hair was dark but naturally curly and her figure was, she was often being told, perfect.

She was well aware that an English Countess was someone of great social stature.

All her American relations, when they heard of the engagement, had written her glowing congratulations and sent her bouquets of flowers.

A number of them were very envious that she had been clever enough to make herself so important on both sides of the Atlantic.

As her father had, when he died, been a millionaire, they always expected that Mildred would make a brilliant marriage.

But this was even more brilliant than their wildest dreams.

In all the letters she received from them they were obviously very much impressed by her grand new position in the social world.

But there was also a note of resentment that she had jumped so far ahead of them.

'I have won! I have won!' Mildred said to herself every night before she married.

There was a note of awe in her voice when she first saw The Manor House as they drove through the beautiful countryside that her husband told her was all his as well as the many fields stretching up to the horizon.

It was when she met Julia that she had a surprise and a shock which felt considerably unpleasant.

There was no doubt that Julia was very lovely.

Her long fair golden hair seemed to be part of the sunshine.

Her large blue eyes resembled the forget-me-nots in the garden.

Her pink and white skin, that was the envy of every woman who saw it, was something that Mildred had not expected at all and was therefore not prepared for it in any way.

"Is this your daughter!" she exclaimed.

"Julia is very like her mother," the Earl answered. "She has just become the *debutante* of the year and we are, of course, very proud of her."

It was with some difficulty that Mildred managed to be polite to her.

Julia was well aware that what she said with her lips did not match the expression in her eyes.

She had known instinctively that the woman who had taken her mother's place not only disliked but resented her.

It was as if a dark cloud blotted out the sunshine that she had always felt in her home.

There was no doubt that after being so depressed and so miserable at his wife's death, the Earl was pleased and delighted with his new wife.

He took her round The Manor, showing her all the fine paintings in the Picture Gallery.

He showed her the huge ballroom and all the other parts of the house that had been added every century until they were undoubtedly not only impressive but very large for two people to not feel that they were belittled by them.

"It's really, really lovely!" Mildred kept saying.

At the same time Julia, when she was near to them, realised that she did not miss all the cracks in the ceiling, which were getting worse every year.

Nor the rooms needing repapering and the mullion windows where the panes were cracked or broken.

'I should be thankful,' she had said to herself when she was alone in her bedroom, 'that now these things can be done and paid for.'

But she was too astute not to realise that, while the new Countess was quite prepared to spend her money on

11

the house and on her husband, she certainly would resent every penny that was spent on her stepdaughter.

'I want Papa to be happy and I know that I should be grateful that many things will be done to the house that should have been done years ago,' Julia muttered to herself when she was alone in the night in the still quietness of her bedroom.

But it was difficult not to see the resentment if not hatred in her stepmother's eyes.

'I really ought to go away,' she thought to herself, 'but where can I go?'

But then the mere idea of leaving the garden and the lake that she loved so much and being, even for a short time, with other members of her family, made her shiver.

They had certainly been kind enough when she was in London and she knew that they were delighted that she was such a social success at her 'coming out' ball.

At the same time they had families of their own and they had no wish to enlarge their responsibilities by having Julia attached to them.

'They might,' she thought to herself, 'invite me for a weekend or perhaps a week if there was some particular event like a Race Meeting or a cricket match taking place in their neighbourhood!'

But they would only ask her for a very short time and, although she would certainly enjoy being with them, they would not want her to stay any longer.

Julia was aware of her stepmother's feelings, but it was obvious that the Earl had no idea about them.

"It's very nice for you, my dearest," he said to his daughter the following morning when they were out riding together, "to have someone very near your own age."

He smiled at her.

"Of course now that we can afford them, there will be not only improvements made to the fabric of the house but more horses to ride."

He paused before he added,

"Mildred is already talking of me having a Racing Stable at Newmarket, which would be absolutely thrilling, as you well know."

"Of course it will be, Papa," Julia had agreed.

At the same time she had known only too clearly that Mildred would not want Julia taking any part in the alterations to the house or coming to any festivities that might be given if their horse won the Gold Cup at Ascot or some other enviable prize.

It was so obvious that she would soon make every effort to keep her out of the way when anything unusual occurred.

'She will not want me present when people call on Papa's new wife,' Julia said to herself.

She was most sensitive where other people were concerned and had always been so since she had been very young.

She could well recall the time when her younger brother had been born.

Everyone had come to the house with flowers and congratulations and her mother had thanked her afterwards for taking over the duties of the hostess that she had, for the moment, not been able to do herself.

"You were splendid, darling," she said, "and it is something you must always do when I cannot do it myself. After all, this is your home as well as mine."

Julia had been so pleased at her mother's thinking that she had done the right thing.

But she knew, almost as if it was written in front of her in large letters, that her stepmother would want her out of sight.

Of course she had to stay well away while she was receiving her father's friends, who would undoubtedly call more out of curiosity than if they were genuinely pleased at him having married again.

'Mama was so polite,' Julia thought to herself, 'that Mildred will never be able to take her place in the same way. She will also resent anything I do.'

She had sighed when she thought about it.

She felt as if there was suddenly a dark shadow at The Manor, which had never been there before.

Now, as she knew that she was at fault at being late for breakfast, she hurriedly changed her shoes.

She glanced quickly at herself in the mirror and saw that her hair, which curled naturally, was firmly tied.

It only looked a little windswept over her forehead.

Then she ran swiftly downstairs hoping that as her stepmother had left the dining room she would not then go back.

It was with relief that she found the dining room empty.

The old butler, as soon as he saw her appear at the door, hurried off to fetch the eggs and bacon that he had been keeping warm for her.

Julia sat down at the table.

As she expected, a few minutes later he came back from the kitchen carrying a plate and set it down on the table in front of her.

"You're late, Miss Julia," he said, as though she was not aware of it.

"I know, Bates," she answered, "but it was such a lovely day and I was very thrilled to find that there were small ducklings swimming on the lake."

"They must have hatched in the night," Bates then answered.

"That is just what I thought myself," Julia replied. "There are six of them, which will delight Papa. I suppose he has had breakfast by now?"

"Seven o'clock on the stroke," Bates told her, "then his Lordship were off. He were smiling this morning and I knew he was thinking that soon there'll be more horses in the stables than there's been for the last year or two."

Julia knew that this was true because her father had talked of going to Tattersalls last night at dinner.

She had been excited too, because she knew that the horses they were riding were getting old and there was now plenty of room for a number of new thoroughbreds if they could afford to buy them.

"Madam tells me this morning," Bates said, as he poured out some coffee for Julia, "that I was to have four footmen here. But then I says to meself that be exactly the number of uniforms as be waiting up in the attic for the last ten years."

Julia smiled.

It had always been a sore point with Bates that he did not have enough footmen in the house. But her father had been unable to afford them.

It was only when they had visitors that they hired boys from the village who Bates had trained over the years and who had fitted themselves into the uniforms waiting up in the attic.

"Four footmen!" Julia exclaimed. "Well, you will certainly have a job training them all. But it will seem very impressive to have so many waiting on us."

"I was just telling her Ladyship who doesn't seem to know our English ways," Bates replied, "that we require night-footmen too, which we gave up years ago. The chair in the hall, padded and comfortable as it be, has always been waiting for them."

Julia grinned.

"Of course it has and I am so glad for your sake that we are getting back to the way the house looked when my grandfather was alive. You have told me often enough how many servants he employed at that time."

"Them were the days," Bates agreed. "I were only a young'un when I comes here, but I soon learnt and your grandfather said I were the best footman he had ever had. That was why when the old man retired I then became the butler."

He spoke with a satisfaction that Julia had heard often enough before.

But she smiled at him as if she was listening to it all for the first time.

"What a wonderful butler you have been, Bates," she exclaimed. "No one else could have managed as you did single-handed and kept the dining room looking so spic and span and no one realised when they came to the house that we were so understaffed."

"I really did my best," Bates answered. "But now her Ladyship says I can have as many in the dining room and the kitchen as may be needed and his Lordship'll soon make the house just as good as it were when he was a little boy."

He spoke as though it was something that affected him personally.

Julia knew, because he was such a good servant, that he had been involved by their troubles as if they had been his own.

"All I can say now, Bates," she said, "is that if her Ladyship leaves it to you the house will look exactly as it did when you first came here."

"That's what I intend," Bates replied. "Then we can be proud again as we ought to be."

Julia smiled at him.

"Thank you for my breakfast, Bates, and I do hope that her Ladyship will find something I can do to make this house as beautiful as it should be and just as enchanting as it was when it was first built many, many centuries ago."

Then, rising from the table, she walked towards the door.

She realised that already Bates seemed younger and he was now clearing away breakfast as if he was a young footman instead of an old butler of nearly seventy.

'Money! Money!' she mused. 'It is always money that makes all the difference. Perhaps Papa did the right thing after all in putting someone else in Mama's place as he has done.'

When she first realised that he had married again, she resented it.

Then she told herself that she was being selfish.

The most important thing was for her father to be happy.

As happy as he had been with her mother.

But was that possible?

Could any man, who had been so blissfully happy with someone as lovely and as adorable as her mother, find another woman to take her place?

Her father had travelled to France looking old and rather decrepit.

But he had come back with what she thought was an air of new youth and vigour.

He was obviously very pleased, if that was the right word, with his bride.

There was no doubt from the way she spoke to him that she was delighted with him, with the house and with her new position as a Countess.

'The only cloud in the sky,' Julia thought to herself, 'is me!'

She had now reached the door when Bates looked up from the table.

"I nearly forgot to tell you, miss," he began, "that her Ladyship said, when you'd finished your breakfast, she wanted to see you and I thinks she be in the study, as the drawing room's being repapered."

"Yes, of course," Julia answered him. "She said last night that is what we will use for the time being."

She went out shutting the door behind her and then walked down the passage.

Only as she neared the study, which was where her father had always said that it was one of the most attractive rooms in the house, did she feel her feet slowing, because she had no wish to hurry to her stepmother or indeed for that matter to see her at all.

She had been so happy down by the lake.

She felt now that it would only make things more difficult if she was ticked off, as she expected to be, for being late for a meal.

For a moment she contemplated that she would go to the stables and ride to find her father.

Then she told herself that there was little point in running away.

What had to be said, had to be said, and the sooner it was over the better.

At the same time she knew that her stepmother had brought into the house something that had never been there before.

It had been a kind of resentment and a desire not to mix with each other but to stay alone.

Always before they had wanted to be together.

Her father, her mother, the two boys and her had always seemed happy when they were all together.

They had so much to say to each other and things to discuss and things to tell.

Everything had somehow to be shared because that made it more important and more exciting, as it seemed to be not just part of one person but of them all.

She gave a sigh.

It was no use looking back.

She missed her mother unbearably.

But she sensed that her father was suffering more than she was.

The boys, who had been told the news of what had happened when they were at school, had been distraught at losing their mother who they loved so much.

'It has all happened,' Julia thought to herself, 'and it's no use crying about it. Crying will not bring my Mama back. Therefore, we must think of the future and cling to each other because we still have Papa and he has me and his sons.'

Never for a moment did she think that there would be an interloper.

Someone who was not one of them.

But now her father's new wife was here and she must make the best of it whatever happened.

She reached the study door, but it was closed.

For a moment she thought that she would not go in and be alone in the room with her stepmother.

Instead she would run back to the lake to see the small ducklings, sit in the sunshine and be happy.

As happy as she had been every day since she had been born.

Then she told herself firmly that she would not be a coward.

It was something that had to be faced.

Whatever her stepmother might say to her, she had somehow, for her father's sake, to accept it.

With an effort she put out her hand and turned the handle of the study door.

CHAPTER TWO

When she entered the room she saw her stepmother, not as she expected sitting at the writing desk, but standing in front of the fireplace.

It was almost the same way that her father stood when he had something significant to say to his family or to his friends.

Julia closed the door behind her and slowly walked towards her stepmother.

"Sit down!" the Countess ordered in a sharp and rasping voice.

It told Julia all too clearly that this was not going to be a pleasant conversation.

However, she did as she was told and seated herself on one side of the sofa and then looked up expectantly at her stepmother.

She had to admit that the Countess was extremely attractive in her own way.

But, as she had noticed before, her eyes were hard and unsympathetic.

There was an expression in them that Julia tried not to be frightened of.

"I want to talk to you, Julia," the Countess began, "because for some time now I have been aware that it is not possible for two women to be in this house while your father has so much to do to it."

Julia looked at her in surprise.

"Two women," she said. "Are you suggesting that I should go away?"

"What I have been thinking is more sensible than sending you to your relations or sending you abroad," the Countess replied.

Julia drew in her breath.

This was going to be rather more frightening than she had expected.

In fact she might have guessed that sooner or later her stepmother would want to be rid of her.

"As I have already said," the Countess went on, "it is impossible for two women to be in this house when there is so much to do."

There was a disagreeable scowl on her face, which made her look ugly, as she continued,

"Quite frankly I married your father to be alone with him. I did not expect that at every meal you would be there. In the evenings when I want to talk to him, and I am certain that he wants to talk to me, you are there too as an audience."

The Countess paused.

Then Julia asked,

"So you are now suggesting that I should go away from my home?"

"I have a better idea than that," her stepmother said. "In fact it is something that you should have thought about yourself and that it is time you should have a home of your own."

Julia looked thoughtfully at her for the moment, not understanding.

She was puzzled that she should be so anxious for her to leave everything that had been hers since she had been born.

"Are you really sending me away – for ever?" Julia stammered. "And just where do you suggest that I should – go?"

Despite her effort to speak quietly and sound brave, her voice trembled on the last word.

"What I am suggesting," her stepmother said, "will certainly be to your advantage. It will give you what I feel every woman really wants and indeed craves for and that is a home of her own."

Julia looked puzzled.

She did not understand.

Then her stepmother said almost harshly as if she was thinking that Julia was being rather stupid,

"I am proposing to you that you should be married and your father agrees with me that no one could be more suitable than one of our neighbours."

Julia gave a little gasp.

But she did not speak and her stepmother rattled on,

"We know that Mr. Mansfield whose estate borders on the South with your father's is an exceedingly rich man and I am convinced that he is also ambitious."

Julia drew in her breath.

She knew, of course, exactly who the Countess was talking about.

Mr. Mansfield had come to the County two years ago, bought the largest house next to theirs and acquired an estate to which he was constantly adding, so as to make his position more omnipotent locally.

He had come to the County with the reputation of being exceedingly rich.

He had certainly shown it in employing a number of people to work on his estate.

He was practically rebuilding his house, which was two hundred years old, which, when he had bought it, was in a somewhat dilapidated state.

Julia had met his only son, Hubert, and thought him to be a dull, rather stupid young man.

However, he appeared at all the local Hunts on the most magnificent horses which it was quite impossible for her not to admire.

As her mother was always most punctilious about calling on the new people of the County, she had called on Mr. Mansfield when he had first arrived.

She had found him interesting in the way that he was a self-made millionaire.

But, as she had said to her husband, it was difficult for him to be accepted by everyone in the County as he had very little in common with them except that he was very rich and money opened most doors.

Julia had remembered her father laughing loudly and saying to her mother,

"You have summed him up most cleverly. At the same time a door is always open to a millionaire and there are many organisations in the County that would welcome his money, if not him."

After that Julia had felt rather sorry for the young man who knew no one locally.

He apparently had a few house parties, which were talked about by her other friends, although her father and mother had not accepted the invitation that had been sent to them.

But now she merely stared at her stepmother as she said,

"I have talked it over with your father and he is aware, as I am, that despite his great fortune Mr. Mansfield is not accepted by the people who he most wishes to know, either here or in London."

She paused before she continued,

"Your dear father has therefore agreed with me that nothing could be any more acceptable than that his money should be spent on a bride for his son, who is one of the aristocracy and who will be welcomed wherever she and her husband wish to go."

Julia looked amazed.

"I don't know what you can be saying, Stepmama," she said.

"Then you must be very stupid or perhaps I am not being as explicit as I should be," her stepmother replied. "I am saying clearly that your father and I think that Hubert Mansfield would make you an excellent husband and you would not only be rich but able to introduce Mr. Mansfield to the people he is most anxious to meet."

For a moment there was silence.

Julia just stared at the Countess.

She felt very concerned that her father should think for one moment that she would stoop to marry any man for his money.

She had no more intention of marrying someone like Hubert Mansfield than flying over the moon.

"I have," her stepmother continued, "discussed this very thoroughly with your father and made him see how excellent the position would be for you. He has therefore agreed to call on Mr. Mansfield either today or tomorrow to talk through the matter with him."

She smiled before she added,

"I am quite certain that he will be overcome with delight. You will not only be the richest girl in the County but will have the support of your father's family, who will be kneeling at your feet in gratitude."

Before Julia could say anything her stepmother said quickly as though she was anticipating what she was about to say,

"I don't wish to discuss this any further with you. Your father has agreed and is making all the arrangements. If you have any common sense, you will be exceedingly grateful to us for planning your future in such an agreeable and, I am quite sure, happy manner."

Julia stiffened.

She had a great deal to say on the subject, but she knew instinctively that her stepmother would not listen to her.

To make a scene she reflected at this very moment would not be to her advantage.

Pressing her lips tightly together to prevent herself from saying everything that came into her mind, she rose to her feet and walked towards the door.

As she reached it, her stepmother, who was quite obviously surprised at her silence, said,

"I am sure, as you have nothing to say in the matter, you are being very sensible. It will please your father and I am quite certain that Mr. Mansfield will be more delighted than he can possibly express in words at such an agreeable and advantageous offer."

She had reached the door and Julia did not look round.

She merely opened it and then walked out closing it quietly, although she wanted so much to slam it as hard as she could.

She ran as quickly as she could up the stairs to her bedroom.

When she reached it, she locked the door.

Taking off the gown that she had put on earlier, she dressed herself in her riding clothes.

With a speed that even prevented her from looking at herself in the mirror, she was dressed and ready to go.

She then opened her bedroom door very gently and listened.

There was no sound.

Just for a brief moment she was concerned that her stepmother might have been coming up the stairs or going to her own room which was on the same floor.

As she was afraid of encountering her, Julia slipped down the backstairs, past the pantry and out by the kitchen door onto the path that led to the stables.

Her father had gone out to luncheon with friends who wished to discuss a meeting which would have to be held.

It was to support their Member of Parliament, who had just made a speech in the House of Commons, which had annoyed the Prime Minister and other Members of the Cabinet.

A groom saddled Julia's horse for her.

She rode away, confident for the moment that her stepmother would have no idea of where she was or where she would be going.

She had the idea, however, that Hubert Mansfield would be riding near the field that bordered her father's land.

It was a flat piece of land with hedges, which made it a really excellent place for teaching and training a young horse to jump.

She had, in point of fact, thought it intelligent of him to realise it.

She had been told that, because he was so rich, Mr. Mansfield was intent on building a private Racecourse on his land.

He was also buying up, with no expense spared, the best thoroughbreds that had come up for sale recently at Tattersalls.

"At least, in that way, if in no other, he will be an asset to the County," she had said to her father when they heard about it.

"He will be an asset in a great number of ways," the Earl had replied. "In fact I don't know of any hospital or charity who would not rub their hands together with much delight at the mere thought of having a millionaire in their midst."

Julia had laughed.

"Perhaps he will not be as generous as they expect, Papa," she answered.

"Then quite naturally we must get him to open his purse," her father had said, "but it may not be as easy as people anticipate."

Although, of course, the situation could be difficult, as those who had lived here for generations were always inclined to turn up their noses at any newcomer unless he had a Family Tree as ancient as theirs.

"I dislike any form of snobbery," the Earl had said.

It was something that her mother had found totally unbearable.

She had always gone out of her way to be kind to the Parson's daughter who had been snubbed by the Squire of the village.

And the young married couple who had settled in a small house where they hoped to be able to have a family, but who were of no great interest to the more important members of the social community.

Riding towards the field where she thought that she might find Hubert, Julia felt her anger beginning to move within her.

How dare her stepmother wish to get rid of her by marrying her to a young man who was undoubtedly very rich?

At the same time his father's Family Tree did not, in any way, equal theirs.

Yet, as her stepmother had been aware, he would be delighted to be associated with the Earl.

Although she did not say it in so many words, Julia was very conscious that her stepmother had really wanted to say,

'If you want money, you must find it for yourself and not expect mine to be always at your disposal.'

It was indeed a really excellent excuse for making her marry the son of a millionaire.

Equally Julia knew that her mother would never, under any circumstances, have expected her to marry any man unless she loved him.

'Nor do I intend to do so,' she determined as she rode on.

It took a little time because their own land reached out in that particular direction.

The ground was now too rough for her to gallop her horse, although she would have liked to do so.

Finally with her father's boundary now in sight, she could look over it and see, as she had hoped, that Hubert Mansfield was, as she had expected, riding his horse over some challenging fences.

It would have been easy to jump the hedge to reach him, but Julia deliberately went to a gate which had never been locked.

This was because no one had ever wished to use it.

With some difficulty because it was broken in parts, she pushed the gate open and rode onto the neighbouring land.

She had not gone more than a short distance when the hedge a little way ahead of her was jumped by Hubert Mansfield.

As he then drew in his horse, he looked at her with surprise.

"I have come to see you," Julia said before he could speak, "on an important matter and I wonder if you could spare only a few minutes of your time to discuss it with me."

Hubert took off his hat and replied,

"I thought it must be you, Lady Julia, but you have never come here before and I was not quite certain if this land is yours or ours."

"As it happens, it is ours," Julia pointed out, "and I think that you will find it a very good jumping ground."

"I thought that too," Hubert agreed. "But of course, if you want to talk to me, we can ride to the stream which as you doubtless know, is just a little way to ride over the next couple of fields."

"Actually I had forgotten it," Julia said. "Because it is such a trickle in our ground, we have never bothered about it."

She did not add that her father had wanted to take it out and make it more useful, but had thought that it was an unnecessary expense and something he could not afford at that particular time.

Turning her horse to walk by the side of Hubert's, they rode slowly towards the stream.

"That is indeed a very fine horse you have," Hubert commented.

"He is my own and I love him," Julia replied. "But I hear that you are buying the best horses available and you will soon be the envy of everybody in this County, who knows about horses."

Hubert laughed.

"I like riding, but my father insists that we should have a stable full of fine horseflesh. So the sooner I can get used to training them the better."

"What would you rather do?" Julia asked him.

Hubert shrugged his shoulders.

He was not particularly well proportioned and he was short compared to many men of his age.

On the several occasions that Julia had met him she had thought him rather backward.

Equally she had tried not to be critical knowing that everyone else in the County was criticising Mr. Mansfield and his son.

They were at the same time hypocritically blessing them because of their huge fortune and telling themselves that it was the only thing that mattered.

They had by now reached the side of the stream and Julia dismounted.

"I think my horse will want to go down to have a drink," she said, "but he will always come back when I whistle for him."

"I would doubt if mine will do the same," Hubert answered, "so perhaps I had better keep my eye on him in case he runs away."

"If he does, I can see your man in the distance and I know he will catch him again," Julia remarked.

"Then I will risk it," Hubert replied.

He sat beside her on the ground which sloped down to the river.

"What do you want to talk to me about?" he asked. "I expect it is something I have to give to the Church or the hospital. People have called on my father every day since we came here. As they go away smiling, I know that he has given them what they want."

"I have something quite different to discuss with you," Julia said. "I know it will be as much of a shock to you as it has been to me."

Hubert took off his hat and turned to look at her expectantly.

He was most certainly a plain young man, but no doubt, she mused, like his father, he could use his common sense.

He would surely understand what she had to say to him.

"I have just been talking to my stepmother," she began, "she dislikes me because she wants my father all to herself. She has no wish, as she said quite forcibly, to have two women in the house at the same time."

Hubert looked at her in surprise.

"Do you mean that you will have to move out?" he asked.

"Yes, that is just the right word for it," she agreed. "But what I do concerns you. I thought that you should know about it before your father tells you why my father is going to call on him."

Hubert looked somewhat bewildered.

Then Julia explained,

"My stepmother has informed me that she and my father have agreed that a marriage will take place between us. But let me say, before we go any further, that I have no wish, Hubert, to marry you."

Hubert stared at her.

Then he said,

"If it comes to that, I don't want to marry anyone. I enjoy being here and Papa has bought a nice bit of English land. I have other ideas of what I want to do, but now I have to stay and train the horses."

There was a note in his voice that told Julia it was something he did not really want.

Then she said quickly,

"What do you want to do?"

"I want to go round the world," Hubert told her. "But my father said that I have to take someone with me and I have been thinking who I could ask."

He spoke almost bitterly and Julia said,

"As I have told you, I have no wish to be married. Therefore we must stand against our parents whatever they have to say on the matter."

Hubert shrugged his shoulders.

"My father always gets his own way," he said, "that is how he has made himself so rich."

"But he would not let you go round the world," Julia remarked. "Was it because it was so expensive?"

"No, not that!" Hubert replied. "He said I could go if I wanted to, but it would be a mistake to go alone. He said I must take a friend with me and it must be someone who does not bore me."

Hubert was silent for a moment.

"The trouble is I asked William Longford to come with me and he said that he could not, although it was something he would very much like to do."

Julia did not answer immediately.

After a moment's pause she said as an idea came to her,

"Did you ask William to go as your guest or did you expect him to pay his own way?"

"I don't know," Hubert replied. "I just asked if he would come round the world with me and he said that he could not."

"What he really meant," Julia said, "is that he could not afford it. But you could afford to take someone with you as your guest and I am quite certain, knowing William, that he would not refuse anything like that."

Hubert thought this over.

Then he said,

"All right, it was stupid of me and I will ask him again."

He paused before he added,

"You said that you did not want to get married. I don't want to get married either. I want to see a great deal more of the world before I settle down in one place as Papa is ready to do."

"Of course you are right," Julia said. "At your age you should see the world and learn a great deal from it. But naturally it will be a very expensive trip and the other person you should invite to go with you will have to go as your guest."

"Do you think if I ask William again, he will say 'yes'?" Hubert questioned.

"I am quite sure he will," Julia assured him. "And I have another suggestion for you. Take Richard Bridgeman with you. He is a little bit older than you are, but he has travelled as much as he can now manage and is a walking encyclopaedia on foreign countries."

She paused for a moment.

"As he has always wanted to travel everywhere," she went on, "but has had to save up for months before he could afford to even cross the English Channel, he has read every book there is on travel in our library and that is saying a great deal."

She smiled at him.

"Also every book he could afford about the East and their history and religions."

"That is just the sort of person I would like to take with me," Hubert replied.

Julia drew in her breath.

"Then what I suggest you do, is to go and see these two men immediately. Tell them it is important that you should leave as soon as possible. In fact tomorrow if you can."

Hubert laughed.

"I doubt if I could do it as quickly as that, but I see what you mean."

"If you don't hurry and get out of the way," Julia told him, "we will find ourselves married whether we want to be or not!"

Hubert giggled.

"I don't want to be rude," he replied, "but quite frankly I don't want to marry anyway until I am so much older. Then I suppose I will have to have an heir to inherit all Papa's money."

"But you have to inherit it all yourself first," Julia pointed out, "and nothing could be better than to have a knowledge of the world as it is. You don't have to travel uncomfortably, you can do it in state."

She gazed at him before continuing,

"At the same time you can see all the things you have wanted to see but only read about in books."

She hesitated before she added,

"It is never the same as seeing them first-hand and alive."

She saw a light in Hubert's rather dull eyes that had not been there before.

"It is what I have always wanted," he said, "but it was not possible when Mama was alive because Papa went off leaving her alone and because she wanted me to be with her I went to a day school for some time so that I could be."

"Then it is only fair that your dream should come true now," Julia told him, "and you can see the world as you have always wanted to see it. But you have to hurry. If your father and mine believe that they can force us up the aisle and married off as my stepmother wants us to be, they will work fast."

"I know exactly what you mean," he said. "When my father has his heart on a new project he wastes no time. That is why he always gets whatever he wants while other people are still talking about it."

"That is what I am afraid might happen now," Julia said. "So I would suggest that you go and see William and Richard and leave as soon as possible. If not tonight, then tomorrow."

Hubert laughed again.

"You might be my father talking. That is the way he always works."

"I know," Julia replied. "That is why I think we might find ourselves up the aisle before we can even draw breath. But if the bridegroom is not there, they can hardly marry me to his memory!"

Hubert chuckled as she had meant him to do.

Rising slowly to his feet he then walked towards his horse.

"I am going to do exactly what you have told me to do," he said, "and, as I know that my father has to go to London tomorrow for a meeting he will not wish to miss, the best thing I can do is to have started on my travels by the time he comes home."

Julia clapped her hands.

"That is very clever of you, Hubert, and exactly what I know is right for you to do."

"What are you going to do?" Hubert quizzed her.

"I too am going to disappear," Julia told him. "I have had enough of being ordered around when I least expect it. While you are going round the world I have been thinking that I might go to Scotland where some of my mother's relatives live. They might be pleased to meet me and let me stay with them for a short while."

"That sounds sensible," Hubert commented.

"The trouble is actually getting to Scotland," Julia sighed, almost as if she was talking to herself.

"I can tell you how to do it!" Hubert exclaimed.

"How?" Julia asked him.

"Well, I knew of a man who wanted to sell me his yacht. It is quite a big one and, although I did not want it, as he was so pressing and he needed the money, I bought it from him."

Julia did not reply and he went on,

"He has it anchored in the River Thames. He keeps writing to me to ask me to go with him to Scotland as he thinks I will enjoy the journey and meet new people I have never met before."

He stopped for a moment and then continued,

"He was just tempting me with words after I had bought the boat from him, but I thought that it would be a rather boring journey and I prefer training the horses than doing what he asked."

Julia drew in her breath.

"Are you telling me that I can have the yacht and go to Scotland in it?" she asked him.

"Of course you can," Hubert answered. "You have saved me and given me the opportunity of seeing the world which has always been a chance I have wanted more than anything else. As this boat belongs to me, the man who was the owner is prepared to stay on and run it for me and he would have to do what I tell him."

He thought seriously for a moment longer and then said,

"I will drop him a note telling him that you are my guest and he is to look after you and do what you want until you return here and I come back home."

Julia clasped her hands together.

"You are kinder than I believed possible," she told him. "I can only thank you for saving us both from being unhappy for the rest of our lives."

Hubert smiled.

"Let's hope that nothing will go wrong at the last moment," he said. "I will go off abroad while Father is in London tomorrow and you can pick up *The Mermaid*. It is anchored near the Tower of London and I will write a letter to him and send it by hand to you tonight telling him what he has to do and you can give it to him when you get to London."

Julia wanted to say 'if I get to London,' but thought that it would be a mistake.

Hubert had been so positive that she did not wish to have to raise any doubts in his mind.

He was ready to go away abroad tomorrow and she admired him for making such a big decision so quickly.

In that way he somehow resembled his father.

At the same time she knew, without anyone telling her, that she would hate to be married to him.

If they were constantly together, there would be no happiness for either of them.

'I will not marry anyone,' Julia thought, 'unless I am in love with the man in the same way that Mama was in love with Papa. They might well have been made for each other, they were so happy together.'

She rose to her feet.

"I think, Hubert," she said, "that you are being very wise and very clever about this. If we move swiftly, no one will be able to stop us."

"No one will be able to stop me," Hubert boasted. "I am going off to see William at once and then Richard afterwards."

"I am sure that they will be delighted to accept your invitation," Julia said. "But you must tell them that our movements are secret until we are both out of reach of our parents."

"I will tell them that and I am quite certain that they will believe me," Hubert said. "Anyway the sooner we get going the better. I will send you the letter for the Captain of *The Mermaid* as soon as I go back and make quite sure that he takes you where you want to go."

"Thank you! Thank you!" Julia cried.

After she had spoken, she whistled for her horse, who came trotting up to her.

She then sprung onto his back without waiting for Hubert to assist her, which he had not thought of doing anyway.

Then she said,

"Goodbye and good luck and don't let anyone stop you!"

"No one is going to," Hubert answered. "And it is the most exciting thing that has ever happened to me."

Julia was moving off as he was speaking.

She reflected with a smile that many men would have thought it exciting to marry her, but certainly Hubert had other ideas.

Now she had to get ready to go to London.

It was so essential that her father should not realise that she was leaving until she had actually gone.

As for her stepmother, she felt, as she rode home, that she would be delighted if she disappeared.

If she left a letter saying that she was going off to Scotland to meet her relatives and, when her father found that there was no sign of Hubert either, everything to do with the marriage would be postponed until they had both returned.

As she then rode towards The Manor, Julia thought about what she would need on her journey.

She reckoned that the most important thing was to have enough money.

She had been worried about money ever since her mother had died and she had taken over the running of the house.

It was only then she realised how difficult things had been simply because the treasures of The Manor were entailed so that they could never be sold.

Her father had most definitely been unable to pay the servants what they deserved or to keep his horses fed until he had married her stepmother.

'I should be grateful to her for what she is spending on the house and grounds and what a difference being rich will make to Papa,' she said to herself. 'At the same time I will not let her run my life or, as she wishes to do, get rid of me by marrying me off to Hubert.'

Even as she thought of Hubert, she knew that she could not bear him to touch her and she winced at the very idea of him kissing her.

It was not that he was actually repulsive.

It was that she knew in her heart that she would never, never marry unless she could find real love.

The love that had made her father and mother so happy.

It had made their home, penniless though it was in one way or another, a place where two people were utterly content at being with each other.

"That is what I want and that is what I am going to have," Julia said firmly to her horse as she rode into the stables.

She had a feeling, although it might be imagination, that her mother was smiling at her.

CHAPTER THREE

By the time that Julia had changed her clothes for luncheon, her father had returned.

She heard him talking to his wife, who had run out of the study to welcome him.

Julia guessed, although she was not certain, that her stepmother would tell her father what had happened during the morning.

How Julia had just walked out of the study without saying a single word.

If she had been clairvoyant, she would have heard her stepmother saying,

"I am sure, my dearest, that she will obey you when you tell her what she has to do. But I do think that it would be wise of you to see Mr. Mansfield first and discuss it all in detail."

"I am seeing him this afternoon," the Earl replied. "There is a meeting called by the Master of Foxhounds and I am sure, unless he is away, that Mansfield will be there too ."

"Well, you must take him on one side and then tell him that you want to have a serious conversation with him where you will not be interrupted," the Countess told her husband.

She smiled at him as she continued,

"It is very important that he is enthusiastic about the idea and, as I might have expected, we may have a little trouble with Julia."

"Trouble?" the Earl questioned. "You mean that she will not want to marry the boy?"

"You know what girls are like," his wife answered. "They like to make a big fuss before they agree to anything and I expect that is what Julia will do."

She paused.

"You have to be firm with her," she continued, "but as I said before, I should talk to Mr. Mansfield first. Then, when he is full of enthusiasm and delight at the idea, as I am quite sure he will be, that will be the moment to tell Julia that it is all arranged and agreed."

"I expect that you know best," the Earl said a little dubiously.

He had learnt already that when his wife talked on and on about something, it was best to agree quickly and then change the subject.

"Now let's go into luncheon," he suggested. "I am very hungry and so much looking forward to the excellent food that the cook is now giving us."

"She is delighted, I may tell you, at being able to order the most expensive ingredients that are available and I feel that you must have suffered many days of scraps and rubbish until I came here," the Countess replied.

The Earl wanted to tell her it was not as bad as all that.

But her money was the subject that always made him feel slightly embarrassed.

He therefore walked towards the dining room door saying as he did so,

"I see that you have on a dress you have never worn before, which I don't have to tell you makes you look even more beautiful than you do already."

His wife smiled at him.

"This is the sort of compliment I like to receive," she said. "I feel sure that, as Englishmen are very bad at compliments as a rule, it is what they taught you to do in Paris."

"They did teach me a lot," the Earl laughed. "You must admit that the moment I saw you I knew you were one of the most beautiful women I had ever seen."

His wife noticed that he paid her his compliments in the plural, but thought it best not to mention it.

Instead she slipped her arm through his and said,

"It is lovely to be here and this afternoon I want to show you the improvements I think we should make to the ballroom."

The Earl raised his eyebrows.

"Are you thinking of giving a ball?" he enquired.

"If not a ball, we must have large parties here. I know a number of people in London are longing for us to ask them to stay as they are so curious about this wonderful house of yours and the treasures it contains."

"There is a great deal more to be done," the Earl said, "before I want to show it to anyone. But, of course, dearest, you must make your plans. Only give me a little breathing space before the house is to be packed with our London friends who will undoubtedly be, if nothing else, highly critical."

The Countess laughed.

"They will not dare to be critical to me and if they are then it will be the last time they are asked to cross the threshold!"

Then they were both laughing.

Having overheard most of this conversation from the dining room door, Julia now entered the room.

She then recognised instinctively by the expression deep in her father's eyes when he looked at her that he was

44

wondering if she was upset by what she had been told or if she was, as he hoped, now ready to accept the situation and agree to marry Hubert Mansfield.

"Have you had a busy morning, Papa?" Julia began as she sat down beside him.

He did not answer immediately and she went on,

"I know you will be thrilled to hear that there are a number of baby ducklings on the lake. When I was riding through the orchard I saw no less than three hen pheasants which must have come to us from our neighbours' woods because as you know, last year we had so few of our own here."

She did not add that they could not afford to buy more.

But she knew it was what her father was planning to do for the autumn.

"Now before you start talking sport," the Countess interrupted, "let me tell you that the builder came an hour or so ago to look at the fountain on the lawn."

She paused before she went on,

"Although he said that a great deal will have to be done to restore it to what it was originally, he hopes to get it to work in about two weeks."

The Earl turned towards his wife and put his hand over hers.

"That is very kind of you, my dearest," he said. "I have loved that fountain since I was a small boy and it broke my heart when it could no longer throw its water up in great spouts towards the sky."

He looked thoughtful as he added,

"It is over three hundred years old and once it is restored it will be one of the most beautiful features to be seen when we have visitors to The Manor."

"We will not only have visitors, but I am afraid that foreigners will love to come to view your pictures and, of course, your wonderful collection of fine old books," the Countess replied.

She paused before she went on,

"I am hoping that the experts I have been in touch with on both these matters will be coming here within a few days."

"I don't know if I am on my head or my heels," the Earl remarked. "But it is very exciting to know that The Manor will be restored to the beauty it was always famous for. I feel that I can never thank you enough. Just like the Queen of the Fairies you have touched us with your magic wand!"

"You know that I would do anything to make you happy," the Countess purred in a beguiling voice.

Julia took no part in this conversation, but ate her luncheon in silence.

She told herself that she should be very pleased that her father was so happy.

Happy that so many things were being changed so that the house would look as splendid as it had a hundred years ago.

Equally she could not help wishing that her mother was sitting in the chair now occupied by the new Countess of Westwood.

And that there was now, as there never had been before, a butler and ten footmen to wait on them.

'I am so ungrateful! I know I am ungrateful!' Julia said to herself. 'But I will not let my stepmother get rid of me by marrying me off to a young man who is a newcomer to the County. Just as I know very little about him, Papa knows nothing about his father, except that he is extremely rich!'

She felt, if anything, that it was a gross insult that she should be pushed away so easily.

And to make it far worse neither her stepmother nor her father were considering her feelings in the marriage in any way.

When luncheon was finished, her father said to his wife,

"I have some letters I must write, but they can wait until later. Would you like to come driving with me? I want to show you a little of the lovely countryside as well as the villages that belong to me."

"I would love it," the Countess replied. "Just wait until I fetch my hat and parasol in case we have to walk in the sunshine!"

"I will see that the carriage is waiting for us as soon as you are ready," the Earl smiled.

The Countess hurried away.

As they left the room, the Earl turned towards his daughter.

"I am not asking you to join us, Julia," he began, "simply because, as you will realise that your stepmother likes being alone with me. I am sure that you can find something amusing to do. If I was in your place, I would go swimming in the lake."

Julia grinned at her father.

"Don't worry about me, Papa, I have plenty to do and, as it is a lovely day, I might swim, as you have just suggested."

"I wish I could join you," he replied. "But you can understand that I don't want your stepmother to get bored in the country. After all she was always very busy when she was in Paris and was entertained from breakfast until dinner almost every day."

Julia gazed at him.

"I am quite sure, Papa, that she will be very happy driving with you and very proud that you own so much land and are so closely connected with the people who live on it."

"Very concerned indeed," the Earl said with a sigh. "It's hard to believe that now I can help them, as I always wanted to do. As I told the Vicar of Newland, who I saw today, that he should start to repair the door of his Church immediately."

"I am sure he was thrilled to hear the good news," Julia said.

"He was indeed. In fact he stared at me as if he thought that I was pulling his leg. Then, when he saw that I was serious, he was as delighted as if he was a small boy being given a large piece of chocolate!"

Julia laughed.

But she knew that her father had been desperately worried about the people in his Parish.

There was not one who did not require repairs to be done to the schools and the Churches. And the cottages on the estate were in an even worse state.

Julia waited until her father and his wife had left in the carriage.

Then she hurried up to her bedroom and started to pack everything that she thought she would need when she was travelling to Scotland.

She had just a few clothes of her own, but she also packed those which had belonged to her mother knowing that she would not only need them but be glad that they were hers.

She filled her two cases and a hat box in under an hour.

Then she went to her writing desk to write a letter to her father.

This was most difficult and she sat wondering what she should say, having no wish to hurt or antagonise him.

At the same time, being aware that she had to make it very clear that she had no wish to marry anyone, least of all Hubert.

Finally she wrote,

"*Dearest Papa,*

I am going away because I want to think over what Stepmama has told me.

She says that you wish me to marry and I should now make myself scarce for at least a short time.

I have therefore decided to travel to Scotland and meet some of Mama's relatives who we have corresponded with but never met.

I am sure you will not begrudge me this holiday as I am so looking forward to it.

Please don't worry about me as I am travelling in a yacht with a friend who will look after me.

I will be longing to see the house when I return and I know that the many improvements which are now being made will make you prouder of it than you have ever been in the past.

With so much love, my dearest Papa, and I will be thinking of you on my journey but please, please don't be concerned about me.

Your affectionate daughter,

Julia."

She read the letter through and thought that it said everything she wanted him to know.

She left it on her dressing table where it was certain to be found when her father learnt that she had left the house.

She then carried her cases down to the stable and hid them in a special place that was not being used by the grooms.

She knew that there was no one likely to question them being there.

She then told one of the stable boys, who she knew was a good driver, that she wished to leave for London early the next morning before anyone else was awake.

"I have a long day's journey in front of me, Jim," she told him, "and you know as well as I do, that grown-ups always think that I do too much. They will certainly protest at my going on a long journey without anyone to accompany me."

She hesitated before she added,

"As there is no one able to do this at the moment, my father might well refuse to let me travel with you. But I know, Jim, that you will look after me as well as the horses."

She smiled at him.

Therefore, if you will be ready at five-thirty tomorrow morning before anyone is awake," she continued, "we will leave for London and reach there before the roads become busy and we are held up by the traffic."

The stable boy, who was eighteen years old, had really shown himself to be excellent with their horses.

He was delighted at the idea.

"You do understand," Julia said to make sure, "that you tell no one I am going because we will travel so much quicker if we are only two in the old donkey-carriage than if we had to take one of the bigger carriages."

The old donkey-carriage was very light.

With two of the best horses to pull it, it could reach, Julia knew, quite a good speed and they would be in London before luncheon.

"I'll be ready, my Lady," Jim said, "and I'll tell no one. You can trust me."

"I know I can," Julia replied, "and thank you for being so understanding."

She showed him where she had put her cases and he said in surprise,

"Ain't you comin' back, my Lady?"

"Not tomorrow. I am staying with some friends and I will ask Papa if you can come and fetch me when I have enjoyed house party I am attending."

She paused for a moment.

Then she said,

"In the meantime not a word to anyone! I will be very disappointed if I am unable to go to London and my stepmother might insist on accompanying me in which case you would not be able to drive me as she would want to go in the big carriage in state."

She saw by the boy's face that he would be exceedingly disappointed if this happened.

She knew therefore that he would keep his tongue silent.

She smiled at him and then said in almost a whisper,

"Five-thirty, Jim, and let's hope it's not raining."

Then she walked away.

Now she asked herself intently if she had remembered everything she would need.

Then, almost with a start, she realised that above all, she would require money.

She could hardly ask her stepmother for any.

She was quite certain if she asked her father for a large sum of money he would undoubtedly want to know the reason why.

'What I have to do about this,' she thought to herself, 'is to be clever. I obviously cannot run away with the small sum I possess at the moment. Although Hubert has been kind enough to provide me with transport, I will still, when I leave the yacht, have to buy myself food and accommodation until I find my relatives.'

She sat quietly thinking for some time what she should do.

Then she went to her father's favourite sitting room where his writing desk was.

She was not mistaken in thinking that at the back of one of the drawers there would be his cheque book.

In fact there were three of them.

One was for his personal expenses and the second for the household.

The third was for exceptional payments which concerned pictures and other items of value that were all entailed.

After some consideration she took her father's personal cheque book which actually had hardly been used.

She opened it in the middle and wrote a cheque for five hundred pounds which she signed, copying closely her father's signature so well that she knew the Bank would not question it for a moment.

As she closed the cheque book, she thought that she was not depriving her father in any way.

Her stepmother was determined to make the house as fine and as impressive as anyone could possibly want and Julia thought that no one could make a mistake in thinking that she was not the Countess.

Therefore, the Palace in which she found herself had to be as grand as she wanted and needed it to be.

In fact she was not actually concerned with the feelings of those who lived there, but the compliments and appreciation which would flow into it because it was so spectacular and awe-inspiring.

'She can be the Queen of the Palace, just as she wants to be,' Julia thought. 'But then she is thinking of herself and not of Papa.'

She could not help but recall that her mother had never glorified at being the Countess of Westwood.

But she had done everything that she could, under very limited conditions, to make her father proud and happy, as he had indeed been.

Putting the cheque book back in its place and, knowing that her father would not find out what had happened for some time, she hurried upstairs.

She wanted to be quite certain that she had left nothing of use behind and had packed everything that she was likely to need.

This would prevent her from spending any of her money unnecessarily, but only what was really essential to keep herself alive.

She had finished everything that she thought she ought to do, when she heard her father and stepmother returning from their drive.

It was fortunate that on that evening they had agreed to dine with a neighbour who was most anxious to meet the new Countess.

She had begged the Earl to bring her over that evening because her son and his wife, who lived in London, would be staying for the weekend.

There was no invitation for Julia, which made it very much easier for her than it might have been.

In fact Bates brought her dinner on a tray and she ate it in the sitting room.

"Are you quite sure that you'll be comfortable here, my Lady?" he enquired anxiously.

"Much more comfortable than if I had to sit at the big table in the dining room with you and your new footmen waiting on me," Julia replied.

Bates laughed.

"Things be changed, my Lady, to what they were," he commented.

"And they will change even more in the future," Julia said. "The house is going to look as beautiful as when it was first built and you will be finding people hammering on the door almost every day to ask if they can look round it."

"I hopes not," Bates retorted. "I'm getting old and my feet find the stairs hard going when I go up and down them more than once or twice a day!"

"Then you must train the footmen to take them round until we have the right sort of people who will be able to explain the date and artist of every picture and the date of the furniture, the silver and the china."

Bates laughed again.

"And so what will you be doing, my Lady, when that happens?" he asked.

"I will find something to do," Julia said, and you are not to worry about me or to let Papa do so. I can look after myself and it is something I might well have to do quite frequently in the future."

She dare not say any more.

But she knew that Bates would tell her father she could look after herself when he was worried that she had left home without giving any warning.

It was only when she went to bed that night that she thought perhaps she was taking a very outrageous step in going off on her own without her father's permission.

But she had no alternative because she was quite sure, if her stepmother found that Hubert had vanished, she would find someone else equally unattractive.

Although perhaps not quite as easy to manage as he had been.

In fact it might be a man who would consider it useful to his ambitions to marry the daughter of an Earl.

If he was agreeable, it would be even more difficult for her to say 'no' and run away than she was managing to do at the moment.

'I think it is God who has shown me the way out,' Julia said to herself. 'Or perhaps Mama is helping me from Heaven itself. After all, she would never want me to marry anyone I did not love and I know that if I pray hard enough she, as well as God, will help and protect me whatever might happen in the future.'

She told herself this again and again when she was lying in bed.

She had left the curtains drawn back so that she would wake with the morning sun.

Now the moon was throwing a bright silver light into her bedroom.

The moonlight was something that had always moved Julia.

And she felt as if the moonlight was telling her not to be afraid.

'I am not really afraid,' she told herself. 'It is just that I am leaving home and leaving behind everything I have known and loved since I was a child.'

Then she told herself that wherever she was going, her mother would know about it and would somehow guide and keep her from any harm.

'Help me, Mama, help me!' she prayed. 'I know that perhaps you would disapprove of me going off alone. At the same time I know you would not want me to marry a man I did not love and who does not love me.'

As she prayed, the moonlight seemed to come more fully into the room.

When she then opened her eyes, the beauty of it was inexpressible in words.

It made Julia feel absolutely sure that she was doing the right thing.

If she was running away from what was unpleasant, she was stepping into a future where, if she was sensible and clever, she might find everything she wanted in life and perhaps even love itself.

'I am not hurting Papa by going away,' she told herself. 'He now has everything he wants and everything he must have dreamt he would never have. For me it is a new adventure. An adventure into the unknown world that I have never known but which is challenging and essential for me to explore.'

Then, as she gazed at the moonlight, she said softly out loud,

"Help me, Mama, please help me! You always helped everyone you could and now I need you more than I have ever needed you before."

She closed her eyes for a moment.

Then, as she opened them again, the moonlight seemed to turn the whole room into a celestial part of the sky.

To Julia it was a definite answer to her prayer.

*

It was just after five o'clock when Julia awoke the next morning.

The first gentle rays of the sun rising in the East were flickering into the room.

She jumped out of bed and washed and dressed herself in record time.

She put on a pretty dress that she had worn in London. It was one that she had had no reason to wear when she returned to the country.

She thought that it would give her courage as well as make her appear smarter than she usually was.

She arranged her hair in front of the mirror and put on the smart straw hat which she had bought specially to wear with the dress.

Then she picked up her handbag.

Putting her letter to her father on her dressing table, she opened the door a little gingerly.

There was only darkness and silence in the passage.

She tiptoed along it towards the backstairs that led down to the kitchen quarters.

As the kitchen did not usually wake until half-past five, there was still no one about.

Julia then opened the back door and let herself out.

The air was fresh and cool.

She drew in her breath as she walked briskly towards the stables.

She was not surprised to find that Jim was already there and waiting for her.

In fact he had the old donkey-cart and two of the Earl's fastest horses harnessed to it.

He had put Julia's luggage at the back of the cart.

As she stepped in to sit down beside him, without saying anything, he started the horses immediately.

Almost as if Julia had asked the question, he said,

"No one asked me last night what I were doin' and there were no one about this mornin'."

"That is good," Julia said, "so I will be in London before they realise that we are missing."

Jim giggled.

"Not as quick as that, my Lady," he replied, "but I'll do me very best."

What Julia was now holding in her hand as well as her handbag was the letter from Hubert that she had received last night.

Bates had sent it up to her room after she had finished her dinner.

The footman who had brought it to her had not seemed surprised at her receiving a letter at that late time of the night.

He had merely pushed it into her hand saying,

"Mr. Bates told me to bring you this, my Lady. It's just been handed in at the back door."

Julia thanked him.

She knew exactly what it was.

She had not read it then as she had so many other things to do.

Instead she had put it into her handbag along with the cheque for five hundred pounds that she had taken from her father's writing desk.

She felt somehow as if they gave her courage that she needed and took away her last feelings of being ashamed at running away.

'If I had stayed,' she thought to herself as they moved onto the main road, 'I should have argued not only with Papa but with my stepmother and they would not have listened to me if they could help it. They would have argued on and on until they were certain that I would give in to what they required.'

She had tried not to think about this during the night.

But now because she was free and for the moment no one knew that she had disappeared, she felt as if she wanted to sing.

The glory of the rising sun impressed her.

Because she knew that Jim was so intent on driving the horses, she did not talk to him.

They stopped for a quick luncheon at a Public House which stated that they served food.

Julia thought that it would be a mistake for her to go inside.

She therefore held onto the horses whilst Jim bought sandwiches for them both and a fizzy drink, which he told Julia was his favourite.

It was not something that she particularly liked herself, but it was easier for him to bring back two glasses than for her to be difficult and ask for something different.

They only stopped for ten minutes or so.

When Julia had given him the money for what they had consumed, they set off again.

It was two o'clock when they finally reached the centre of London.

By that time the horses were tired and Julia knew that she should not take them any further.

There was a stable near the house where she had stayed with her mother.

So she told Jim to drive her there.

After giving the horses a nice rest, he could then return to the country in the morning.

She had enough money of her own to tip Jim for his services and also to pay for a stable for the horses.

"Don't get into trouble while you are in London," Julia told him, "otherwise his Lordship will be very angry with me for bringing you here."

"I'll be alright, my Lady," he assured her. "I 'as a friend in London and I'll stay with 'im tonight and then go back in the mornin'."

"That is sensible of you," Julia replied. "And please be good as you know how cross they will be with me."

"You can trust me, my Lady," Jim answered.

Julia shook him by the hand and thanked him again.

Then she had her luggage placed in a passing Hackney carriage.

She decided first to go to her father's Bank, which was not far from where the horses were stabled.

When she reached it, she asked to see the Manager and was shown into his private sitting room.

"This is a surprise, my Lady," he began. "I heard that your father had moved to the country, so I did not expect to see you again for some time."

"I am on my way to Scotland," she told him. "My father has given me a cheque for my expenses and felt sure that you would cash it for me, as I may be away from home for some time."

As she spoke, she handed the Manager the cheque for five hundred pounds.

"Will you be carrying all this money on you, my Lady?" he asked. "I am just thinking it might be safer if you had half in cash and the other half as a cheque."

"I would rather have it all in cash," Julia said, "for the simple reason that I will be moving about. I am going to visit my mother's relations and, as I am not certain how long I will be staying with each one, it will be a nuisance to have to find a Bank to cash the cheque instead of being able to pay my way, so to speak."

The Bank Manager laughed.

"I will be surprised, my Lady, if you have to do that. But, of course, if you prefer cash, I will see to it immediately for you."

He went to the door and gave the cheque to an assistant who was waiting outside.

Julia gave a little sigh of relief.

She had been half-afraid that as she was young he would insist on speaking to her father before he gave her such a large sum of money.

"Now do tell me how you are travelling?" the Manager asked, as his assistant hurried away with the cheque.

"I have been very lucky and I am going by sea," Julia answered. "It is something I have always longed to do and a friend of mine is taking me."

"Then I am sure you will enjoy every moment of it, my Lady. I hope you will be well looked after."

"I am sure I will," Julia replied. "I have always wanted to go to Scotland and never had the chance until now."

The Bank Manager was obviously no longer inquisitive.

He then handed her the money, which she put away in her handbag. He shook her hand warmly and wished her *Bon Voyage.*

Julia thanked him.

Climbing into her Hackney Carriage which was waiting outside she gave the driver the address that Hubert had written down in his letter.

When she opened it up, she had found that there was a letter to the man who owned the yacht as well as a letter to her.

It told her the man's name and he hoped that she would enjoy the journey.

Julia gave the driver the instructions to find a yacht that was called *The Mermaid*.

As Hubert had told her that it was anchored near the Tower of London, they drove along the Embankment.

Julia gave a cry when she caught sight of a rather large and impressive yacht whose name was painted proudly on the bow.

The driver stopped and Julia was relieved to find that it was anchored close to the Embankment.

This made it easy for her to go on board.

She had been half-afraid that the yacht might have been anchored some way out and she would have to signal, although she was not certain how, to the Captain.

It was then that a sailor came forward and asked her what she wanted.

On being told that she now wished to speak to Captain Wood, she was taken to his cabin.

He was sitting comfortably in a leather armchair reading a newspaper.

He looked up in surprise when Julia was announced.

She held out her hand saying,

"How do you do, Captain? I am Lady Julia Westwood and your friend Mr. Hubert Mansfield has given me this letter for you."

"I am delighted to hear from him," Captain Wood said.

He was a man of about forty-five to fifty years of age and Julia thought that he looked exactly as a Captain of a fine yacht should.

He had a sunburnt face and was wearing the clothes that were always connected with a man who went to sea.

He opened the note that Hubert had written to him, read it carefully and then said,

"Mr. Hubert has made it very plain that he will not be accompanying me to Scotland, but, of course, I am delighted for you to take his place as it is a long way to go if you have no one to talk to. I do hope you will enjoy being aboard *The Mermaid*, my Lady."

"I will be thrilled to be at sea," Julia said. "As I have always wanted to travel to Scotland, I can imagine no better way than if you will be kind enough to take me in *The Mermaid*."

"We will then set off as soon as possible," the Captain replied. "I was only waiting because I thought that it would do Hubert good to get away from his father, who is always making him do things he does not want to do, and to travel North which he has never done before."

"Nor have I," Julia told him, "and I am more enchanted than I can possibly tell you to be on this beautiful yacht. It is so kind of you to take me."

"I can hardly refuse Hubert's plea that you should take his place," the Captain answered. "But I hope that it will not be too rough for you and that your first journey to Scotland will be a most enjoyable one."

"I am sure it will be," Julia said. "Please will someone be kind enough to bring all my luggage aboard and to pay the Hackney Carriage."

She gave the Captain enough money to cover what the driver would ask for plus another three shillings as a tip.

The Captain hurried away to give instructions about her luggage.

When he returned, Julia was gazing out of the porthole, watching an assortment of fascinating ships going up and down the River Thames.

"Your luggage is safely aboard, my Lady" the Captain said, "and I sincerely hope that you will find your cabin very comfortable."

"I am sure I will," Julia replied. "I am just thinking how exciting it will be to be at sea and to reach Scotland, which, as I have Scottish blood, should at least make me feel at home with my kith and kin."

The Captain chuckled.

"You must tell me all about it," he said, "and I must find out what Clan you belong to. Now I am going to draw up the anchor and we will say goodbye to London and look towards the North!"

"It is something I have always wanted to do," Julia said, "and thank you, thank you for having me!"

"I should really be thanking you for accompanying me," the Captain replied, "but we will talk about that later."

As he went from the cabin, Julia turned once more to the porthole.

'This is really exciting,' she thought. 'I am going out to explore the country I belong to, but which I have never seen. For a moment I am leaving behind everything which is difficult and running away from what I believe to be the impossible.'

She wondered if her father would be very angry when he realised where she had gone.

But she knew that, although her stepmother might be very annoyed at her being disobedient, she would be delighted to be rid of her.

'At least I am still free,' she reflected. 'At least for the moment I am not tied to anyone and that matters more than anything else.'

CHAPTER FOUR

By the time Julia woke up the yacht was already moving into the sea.

She could hear the waves splashing vigorously against its sides.

She lay in bed for some time thinking how exciting it was to be going off into a strange world which she had never known in her life.

Because Fate had been kind she was not afraid and she had a whole shipful of strong men to protect her against any enemies.

'Not that there will be any,' she mused to herself.

Then instinctively she realised that was just what her stepmother was.

Of course she was an enemy, when she was driving her away from her home.

'This is a world I have never known before,' Julia told herself.

Equally she wanted to look forward to what she would find in the North.

It would be rather embarrassing for her to drop in on her relations of whom she knew very little. In fact she had only met perhaps one or two of them before.

All she knew was that her mother's father had been the Chieftain of a Scottish Clan.

But because her mother had been so beautiful and they were well off, they had brought her to London to be presented at Court. And to meet the other members of her family who were married.

It was shortly after her arrival in London that she had met the Earl.

As she so often told her daughter, they had fallen in love with each other the moment they met.

When she danced with him, she knew that he was part of her dreams.

"Your father always said that the minute he caught sight of me he knew that I was the woman he had been looking for all his life. You do know, my darling, how happy we are and how everything seems so perfect when we are together."

Julia knew that this was very true.

At the same time she wondered if it would ever happen to her.

The few young men she had met were all like Hubert, rather stupid and in her mind unattractive, both physically and mentally.

'Perhaps,' she thought to herself, 'I will meet someone like Papa.'

But her common sense told her that it was one person in a million who found the other half of themselves.

It was her mother who had told her the fascinating story of the Greeks who believed that when God first made a man he was alone and therefore felt lonely and longed for company of any sort.

So they cut him in half and the soft, sweet, spiritual side of him became the woman while he was the fighter, the provider and head of the family which duly followed.

Because she had studied Greek mythology and found it intriguing, Julia knew that the Goddess of Love was someone of great stature in the Pantheon of Gods.

She had treasured what she had read and been certain that one day, if she was lucky, she would meet a man who would be the other half of herself.

Like her father and mother, they would live happily ever after.

'I am doing the right thing in running away,' she told herself over and over again.

She felt that her mother would definitely approve of her doing so.

When the yacht reached the sea, the sun was shining and the water was smooth.

But later in the day the sea turned rough and the yacht, which was not a very large one, began to be tossed from side to side.

"I think we should shelter for the night," the Captain suggested.

He then moved the yacht into the next bay, which was protected by high cliffs and dropped the anchor.

"It has been a very exciting day," Julia told him. "I love being on this wonderful yacht and seeing the sea as one could never see it from the shore."

Captain Wood smiled.

"That is what I want my seamen to feel when they take their first trip with me," he said. "I think you will find that they all love the time we are not resting in Port but moving forward, even if the sea is rough."

When Julia talked to the seamen, she found this to be true.

Although some of them had left behind their wives and children, they still wanted to go abroad and see as much of the world as they could.

They thought that no work could be quite as absorbing as working on a yacht as fine as *The Mermaid*.

Julia could not help wondering if Hubert would enjoy seeing the rest of the world as much as he might have done by going, as his friend wanted him to do, to Scotland.

Then she told herself that Hubert had a great deal to learn.

That was just what he would do when he visited other countries and talked to people of different races and culture.

'I feel as I have read so much about China, Japan, Africa and India that I have actually been to those places,' Julia told herself. 'But, of course, I should learn even more if I really visited them.'

She was delighted to find that there were quite a lot of books on board in a small cabin that was next to the one where she was sleeping.

"Did you collect these books yourself?" she asked the Captain.

"I collected most of them," he replied, "but, when my friends knew what I was looking for, they kindly brought me books from every country they had visited. That is why you will find some very odd volumes on different and intriguing places. Volumes you cannot buy in England, but which are amazingly informative."

It was a temptation that Julia could not refuse under any circumstances.

She soon found herself buried in one of the books that gave a most unusual and intimate impression of China and the millions of people who lived there.

In fact the hours seemed to pass by so quickly when she was either reading or watching the movement of the yacht from the bridge, that they were well on their way North without her realising how fast they were moving.

"Now where actually do you want to go in Scotland?" the Captain asked on the third night of their voyage when she was having dinner with him.

"It will sound ridiculous when I tell you I don't know," Julia answered. "But Mama's relations were mostly in the very North of Scotland. Although I brought her address book with me, I am not certain exactly where they are or if I will have difficulty in finding them."

The Captain chuckled.

"You certainly came away in a big hurry," he said, "but Hubert did not tell me why you wanted to go North and without asking you any unnecessary questions I am rather suspicious that you are running away but for a good reason."

"A very good reason," Julia confirmed. "But it would be a mistake to think about it. But if it is possible I would be most grateful if you would take me to the North of Scotland. I can then start to look round and locate my relatives wherever they may be hiding."

"Alone?" the Captain asked.

"Well, unless you can take your yacht over land," Julia said laughingly. "I have no alternative!"

The Captain was silent.

She thought that he was worrying about her and it was very kind and thoughtful of him.

"I will manage," she said. "I have the addresses of my mother's relations and I will go from one to another and hope that they will ask me to stay for at least a week or two before I have to travel on to the next one."

"You are too attractive," the Captain remarked, "to go about alone. I feel if I sail away as you are advising me to do, I will worry all the time as to what is happening to you and if you are safe and being cared for."

"You are so kind," Julia sighed. "But I promise you I can look after myself, although I am not as old as you would like me to be."

The Captain laughed.

"That is certainly the truth, but let's start with the first one and show me where the nearest harbour is to where *The Mermaid* can anchor while you make sure the relation you are seeking is at home."

Julia handed him her mother's address book, which was full of names, including those who lived locally in the villages on the estate.

"I see that your mother had a cousin here right in the North," the Captain said, "and perhaps it would be wise to take you there. Then I can work down, so to speak, until I get back to England again."

"You are so generous, Captain, and I am most grateful to you."

She was not surprised when two hours later they moved into a bay and she saw that the river running through it created an excellent harbour for passing vessels.

There were only two other ships in the harbour and there was plenty of room for *The Mermaid* to drop anchor near the mouth of it.

"Here we are!" the Captain exclaimed. "I gather your mother's Clan was in this part of Scotland. I am sure that there will be people at the Post Office or greengrocer who will be able to tell you if Mrs. MacCarn is still alive and where she is living at present."

Julia smiled at him.

"You are so kind. I know of no one who would take so much trouble over a stranger and I have loved travelling with you on *The Mermaid*."

She went to the Post Office, as he had suggested, and learnt that Mrs. MacCarn, who she was seeking, had died the previous year.

However, she had a daughter who was married and who lived apparently about two miles to the South of where they were.

"Thank you," Julia said, "you have been very helpful."

She went out of the Post Office and decided that, as it was still fairly early in the morning, she would not return to the yacht.

Instead she asked the way to where she could hire some sort of conveyance.

She was informed that there was a man at the end of the village who hired out his horses to visitors who wanted to see the countryside.

After a while she found his stable, which appeared small and rather inadequate.

The two horses that the man owned were not the sort of horses that Julia was accustomed to at home.

However, as he had an open carriage, she asked him to take her to the South and gave him the address of her mother's relative.

The driver scratched his head.

"I thinks I knows where it is," he asked, "but it's a place I seldom visits."

"Well, we can try to find it," Julia replied hopefully as the man clearly needed encouragement.

"That be true," the Scotsman replied, "but there be a number of people who owns houses there without makin' it clear exactly where they be and it may take us longer than we expects to find this one."

"Well, let's try now," Julia suggested. "If not, there is always tomorrow or the day after."

The man laughed.

"You be an optimist, miss" he said. "But as I said there be a great number of secluded houses in this part of the world and it be right difficult to find some of them."

"I don't want to give up," Julia told him. "Therefore we will just have to keep on trying."

She climbed into the somewhat dilapidated carriage.

The Scotsman then drove his two horses carefully down the winding road that led out of the village.

Soon she was crossing what she thought were the moors and finding them even more beautiful than she had thought they would be.

Because it was summer the heather was just coming into colour.

Julia thought that Scotland was even lovelier than she had ever imagined.

The house they were seeking was more difficult to find than she thought possible.

She soon learnt that the MacCarns were very numerous in this part of Scotland.

Although the driver took her to five different houses where the owner was a MacCarn, as soon as they opened the door she realised they could not, in any way, be her mother's relatives.

After the fifth effort to find her relative, she sat down in the carriage and sighed,

"It seems hopeless! Perhaps I should give up and go back to the yacht."

"There's one man who might know the answer to your question," the driver told her. "He lives in a cottage just to the right of us. We will go down there and ask him if he has any knowledge of the lady you be searchin' for."

"That is a good idea," Julia said. "As he lives nearby, he must know most of the people who have moved here in the last two years."

"I expect he does," the driver replied, "but he's a man who works in the fields and he may not be home yet."

Julia thought that it was worth waiting if this man was not at home.

When they then went down to the small cottage overlooking the bay, she thought that it was so pretty that it would have been a mistake not to see it even if it did not give her the answer she wanted.

When the driver drew up the horses, she jumped out and knocked vigorously on the door.

But there was no reply and after the third time she went back to the carriage.

"I cannot get any answer," she said.

"I told you that Ewen goes out to work," he replied. "We'll just have to wait until he gets back."

"Then I would like to walk a little way along the coast," Julia said. "It's so beautiful here that it is like stepping into an entirely new world and it is certainly one that I have not seen before."

"There be no hurry," the driver declared, "and the horses can rest right here."

Feeling that this was just an excuse, Julia left him and walked along the side of the bay.

When it ended, she turned North and walked beside the sea loving the sound of the waves splashing on the shore and the purple heather coming into bloom at her feet.

Then, as she passed a little hill-top, she saw out to sea on the other side of it, what appeared to be a Castle.

It was, she supposed, about a quarter of a mile from the shore.

Yet it was situated on an island of its own on which she could see that there were several cottages.

It all looked so strange out to sea and yet it was so attractive that she stood still gazing at it.

She sat down on a clump of heather and only wished that she could paint a picture of the glorious scene in front of her.

Then she saw a boat loaded with people coming from behind the island.

She guessed that they must be travellers who had been taken by boat to explore the island, perhaps the Castle on it as well.

She glanced at her watch and thought it unlikely if the man they were seeking was now still at work. Surely he would, by now, have returned home.

'I have time to see The Castle,' she told herself. 'It is something I have always wanted to see, but there never has been one in our part of the County.'

As the boat unloaded a little way from her, she started to walk towards it.

To her surprise she heard some of the passengers talking angrily to the man who had rowed them ashore and gesticulating with their arms.

In fact the men's voices were raised loudly and, as they were talking in broad Scottish accents, she could not exactly hear or understand what they were saying.

She then waited until they had walked away for some distance and the man was alone in his boat.

Next she hurried down the cliff to the place where he had left his passengers.

"Is it at all possible," she asked him, "for me to see The Castle? I thought perhaps the people you have just unloaded were visiting it."

"That's all right," the man replied. "Jump in, miss, and I'll take you out with me in my boat even though you be on your own."

"I just want to see The Castle and it looks so attractive," Julia said.

The man gave a snort as if he disagreed with her, but did not say so.

It only took him a little over five minutes to row her out to the island.

"You gets off here," he said gruffly, "and I'll take you back when you're ready to go, so please come back to this spot on the shore."

Julia then stepped out.

There were a few small cottages on the road, which was rough. In fact, it was difficult to walk on.

But The Castle lay ahead and, because she thought that she ought to hurry, she walked quickly towards it.

It had certainly been very impressive once, but now the windows were smashed and it was obvious that The Castle was a ruin and not lived in.

At the same time she thought that it must have been built many years ago and perhaps it had been the home of the Chief of the Clan who lived in this part of Scotland.

Her mother had once told her how the Clans fought with each other and were continually at war in the past.

They had only ever gathered together and fought side by side against the English, their traditional enemy.

But, because they were ill equipped and had no money to buy decent arms, the English had, in most cases, defeated them.

'I wish I knew more about Scotland,' Julia thought to herself. 'I must now read more books about the country and its peoples than I have already done.'

There certainly did not seem to be any shops in sight as she reached The Castle.

It was then she found that the front door, which should have been impressive, was broken and open.

When she stepped into The Castle, she realised that it was, in fact, almost a complete ruin.

The ceilings must have fallen down and the stairs that led up were broken and very dirty.

'How sad,' Julia thought. 'This must once have been a magnificent Castle, but now it is nothing more than a ruin. I suspect the local people have no money to repair it.'

As she went out of a different door from the one she had entered through, she looked round for the boat that she had come on.

It was then she saw that the cottages which surrounded The Castle were almost in the same dreadful condition as The Castle itself.

But there were people moving about on the island. She saw women washing clothes and the children playing in the sand or rather in many cases the mud.

She thought that they looked thin and rather pathetic and she wondered why this part of Scotland should be so poor.

But there was no time for her to take much notice of the people because she was sure, as she had lingered in The Castle itself and had found it all so fascinating, that the man who had brought her there in his boat would be anxious to take her back to the shore.

She was not mistaken.

"When she reached the little harbour, where she had left him, she found him waiting rather impatiently for her on the top of the cliff.

"You've been a long time," he said reproachfully.

"I am sorry," Julia replied, "but I was so interested in The Castle that I came out on the other side of it and it has taken me some time to walk round."

The man did not say anything, but merely snorted and she quickly climbed into the boat before he pushed it into the sea.

Then he said,

"Now you either gives me all your money or you swims back."

"What did you say?" she asked in amazement.

"You heard what I said and you has a choice," the man snarled. "You can pay me or swim, there ain't no other way of getting back."

He pulled in his oars as he spoke.

"Is this what you said to the other visitors you brought – back from the island?" Julia quizzed him.

"It's what I says to everyone who I may bring here," he replied.

"But – why do you behave like this?" Julia stammered.

He stared at her before he said,

"I don't have to answer that question. You only have to look at the cottages as well as The Castle and the children and the people who lives in them. They'd be starvin' unless I makes some money to keep them alive."

"Why are things in such a bad state?" Julia asked him. "Surely, if you belong to a Clan, the Chieftain is perturbed at the way – his people are suffering?"

The man gave yet another snort, which was really half a laugh.

"He be missin'! We ain't seen him for years! He don't worry about the MacCarns. Why should he?"

Julia remembered what her mother had told her about the Chieftains who led their Clans into battle. They had strict rules about their behaviour when they were not at war.

"I don't – understand," Julia responded.

"You can understand what I tells you," the man asserted. "You pays or swims. Which shall it be?"

Julia drew in her breath.

The large amount of money that she had taken from the Bank was all in notes and she had filled her purse with nearly thirty pounds which she had expected to have spent if she was shopping or buying anything for herself.

Fortunately the rest of the money was secured round her waist.

While she knew that the man would not be aware of it, if she swam in the sea the notes might well be damaged by the water.

At the same time to have to give up five hundred pounds was something she had not anticipated.

She thought again that she would undoubtedly need it if she was to be away from home for a long time.

Aloud she now said,

"Are you telling me that no one has done anything for your Clan and your children, who I could see were very thin and obviously don't have enough to eat?"

"Only what I can afford to buy 'em," the man answered. "Some of the men get work ashore and, of course, I takes them in my boat to the mainland, but they be so weak that in most cases they don't stay very long as they haven't the strength to do what's wanted of 'em."

"It is the most awful story I have ever heard," Julia said. "Someone should speak to the Chieftain of your Clan and tell him just how bad it is."

"Well, you go find him!" the man answered. "He be in Edinburgh or down in England and it be a long way to his Castle and he never seems to be at home."

"So the women and children of the Clan are suffering in consequence," Julia said. "It is the most disgraceful thing I have ever heard. I do wish I could help you."

"No one wants to help us," the man said with a shrug of his shoulders. "We wants food, food to keep us alive, there be no other way."

"But surely there must be plenty of fish in the sea," Julia queried.

"We could fish if we had somethin' to fish with," the man growled. "Most of the men have broken or lost their rods and the hooks which catch the fish are expensive."

Julia knew this to be true.

She thought also that fishing in the sea was not an easy thing to do from an island with cliffs on either side of it.

"There must be something you can do," she said almost as if she was talking to herself, "to help your people, especially the children."

She thought again how thin the little children from the cottages had looked.

She felt that, because her mother had been Scottish, she must help in some way.

"I have an idea!" she exclaimed suddenly. "I want you to take me back to The Castle and call all the men and women on the island to come and talk to me."

The man stared at her.

"Do you mean what you say?" he asked.

"Of course I do," Julia answered. "I want to talk to the people and tell them how they can survive. I must talk to them all because it is something that I feel will be successful only if everyone helps."

There was silence.

She thought for a moment that he was going to refuse her and that was going to insist again on her giving him all her money.

Then she said very quietly,

"I am half-Scottish and am horrified at the position you are in. At least listen to the way I can save you and, while I am doing so, I will give you some money to obtain food, especially for the women and children."

"We men be hungry too," the man pointed out rather poignantly.

Because she had spoken with such conviction, she knew that he was embarrassed by what she had said

"I can help you! I know I can help you!" she insisted. "Please take me back. Only hurry, because I have to return to where I came from and there is a great deal for me to say before I leave you."

Somehow she felt that it was against his feelings of what was right and what was wrong.

But he obviously now realised that she was sincere in her efforts to help him.

"I suppose I must listen to what you have to say," he answered grudgingly. "But if you are kidding, I will want your money or you can swim home!"

"If you are not impressed by what I have to say to you and your Clan," Julia replied, "then I will give you my purse and you shall have what money I have with me."

Her words seemed to reassure the man.

He turned the boat round and started to row back the way they had come.

Fortunately they had not gone very far and it was only a question of minutes before the boat moved into its resting place and she heard the stones crunch beneath it.

She got out, careful not to get her feet wet and climbed up the cliff.

There, straight in front of her, was The Castle as she had seen it earlier. For a moment she just stood gazing at it.

Somehow she then found herself praying to her mother to help her. And to help the people who were in such trouble in her native land.

"Tell everyone and I do mean everyone," Julia told the man, "to come here to listen to what I have to say. I will wait for you on the other side from The Castle, as it is near to the cottages. We only have a little time for me to tell you how you can save yourselves from starvation and deprivation."

"I hopes you're not goin' mad," the man replied, "or I shall look a complete idiot."

"Please hurry," Julia told him, "because if am not home before it's dark the Captain of the yacht, who brought me here will be worrying as to what has happened to me."

Because she spoke so urgently he seemed to realise that speed was essential.

He started to run down to all the cottages which were clustered beneath The Castle.

Because he was shouting at the top of his voice, the women who were hanging out their clothes and the children who were playing came hurrying to listen to him.

For a moment he went on shouting while more people appeared, mostly women, all moving out of their cottages.

Then, as if he convinced them of what he was saying, they started to walk up the small hill in front of them.

Julia moved until she was now sitting on a large stone outside one of the broken windows.

For a moment she wondered if she was doing something really crazy.

Then, as the women walked slowly towards her, all of them thin and emaciated, she knew that what she was about to do was right.

All she had to do now was to tell the people how she could help them with their obvious problems.

The women came nearer and nearer.

It was then that Julia began to speak.

"I am a Scot like you," she began, "and I want to meet you. I feel because my blood is the same as yours that I have to help you and your children."

"If you can 'elp us it'll be a miracle," one woman said. "One of my babies 'as died and the other two are so hungry it looks as though they'll follow 'er."

The way she spoke was almost a snarl.

Then Julia continued,

"I am very sorry that this is happening. It is wrong, so dreadfully wrong that you should suffer like this. That is why I intend to tell you how you can save yourselves and your families."

She was quite certain as she spoke that the women did not believe her. But at the same time they were curious.

As the man was still shouting, and bringing more and more women up the hill, she knew that having gone so far she could not let them down.

She must somehow do what she was determined to do and save these people who were Scottish like herself.

They would, she knew, make her mother cry if she saw how thin they were and how the children were too tired and limp to hurry up the hill.

In fact one small boy sat down and refused to come any further.

Only when his mother and a friend pulled him along by his arms was he able to reach her.

Julia shook hands with everyone who joined them.

All the time the man kept shouting until he reached the end of the houses.

She then found as she looked around that she had an audience of perhaps thirty or forty people.

The majority were women although there were a few old men and a good number of children.

The children, when she told them to do so, sat down on the grass directly in front of her.

The women and the old men completed the circle by sitting on rocks or pieces of wood that must have come from inside The Castle.

There were no chairs and Julia thought that maybe what had once furnished The Castle had been stolen and taken into the cottages.

But these too were in an appalling state of disrepair.

When she looked over the heads of those beneath her, she wondered if she was right in what she intended to do and if she could really help them.

Then she was quite sure in a strange way she could not explain, even to herself, that the answer to her question had come from Heaven itself.

Perhaps it was her mother who was helping her, as they were her mother's people and, as she had said to them, her blood was their blood too.

'I have to do something convincing,' she thought.

Just for a minute it flashed through her mind that she might ask Hubert or even her stepmother for help.

Then she told herself that the Scots were indeed very proud people.

If they wanted to be helped, they would by this time have made other people aware of their distress and, of course, the Chieftain of their Clan.

But their pride had made them suffer rather than make, as most people would have done, a real fuss as to how they were suffering.

She could not help but think that it had been a clever idea for the man who had brought the visitors to The Castle to make them give him their money or swim home, all in a good cause.

She could well imagine the anger of the holidaymakers at having to pay up. At the same time they would undoubtedly be a laughing stock if they explained that they had to swim in the sea to reach the mainland.

Now seated in front of her she was sure that the majority of those living in the broken houses and having little to eat were congregated and prepared to listen attentively to all that she had to say.

At least from their point of view it was something new that anyone cared about them.

She thought, although they did not appear particularly friendly, they were at least curious.

'Help me, Mama! Help me!' Julia prayed.

Then raising her voice, she began to speak.

CHAPTER FIVE

"I am related to you by blood," Julia said, "because my mother was a MacCarn. I am distressed and worried by finding you suffering so greatly and that no one in authority in the Clan has helped you."

She looked round at them.

"What I have to suggest is," she continued, "something that I believe will change your life. And, it will make you proud of yourselves."

She realised that they were all listening to her and no one was moving.

Then she went on,

"As I was coming up the North Sea in a ship I read, and for the first time, some of the history of Scotland. It described most vividly how the Vikings came to plunder and steal from you."

There was silence as she carried on,

"They behaved abominably and then after the first two or three visits, those who were wise on this side of Scotland hid in the hills until they departed."

The people were listening to her and she thought from the expression in their eyes that they had heard all this before and wondered why it affected them now.

"The Vikings must have been impressed by The Castle," she went on, "and they obviously stole from it taking what they fancied and everything of any value."

One or two of the old men nodded their heads as if they knew this to be true, while Julia felt that the women listening to her were becoming rather bored.

"What they must have done after the first two or three visits before they ran to the hills," she said, "was either to take their treasures with them or what was more likely, they hid them in The Castle."

She realised that now the people listening to her had their eyes more intently on her.

She thought that they were sitting up a little higher as if they did not wish to miss anything that she said.

"What I want you to do now," she continued, "and I feel it will be a great help to you all, especially your children because it will bring money to the island, is for the men to dig deeply in the centre of The Castle down to about five or six feet."

She paused.

Then one of the men leaning on a broken wall asked her sharply,

"Why should we do that?"

"I hoped you would ask me that question," Julia replied. "The answer is quite simple. You will see what the MacCarns in the past hid from the Vikings which, as many years have passed since they were here, have now increased in value because they are antique."

"If you ask me," one of the men said, "they didn't have much to leave and I'm certain that they took with them anythin' that was worth a penny piece."

"What I have to say," Julia went on, "is that it does not matter what they left or what they took with them. What we are going to find is a marvellous collection of ancient weapons and anything else that belonged to that turbulent period in history of the Viking marauders."

There was a gasp from some of her audience, while the rest just looked puzzled.

"No one outside this island," Julia said, "must have the slightest idea of what we are doing until we put into the hole dug by the men everything you can spare which is believed to have belonged to the past."

"We ain't got much left," one man shouted. "In fact we 'as no wish to part with any treasure that's 'ere at the moment which may 'ave to be sold for our bairn's food tomorrow or the next day."

"You are not going to lose what is hidden," Julia told him. "I am going to bring everything I can to increase the value and the interest in what your ancestors treasured. As soon as there is enough here to be interesting, I am going to tell the newspapers that we have found a treasure that had been hidden in ancient times."

She paused before she went on,

"I am quite certain that then a large number of curious people will come to view The Castle and its contents."

"You means they 'as to pay to see it?" the man asked, who had brought her to the island in his boat.

"Of course they are going to pay," Julia answered. "I was thinking that, unless they come here in their own boats and require yours, you charge them seven shillings each for the ride and to see the treasure in The Castle."

There was an audible gasp from the audience.

Then she went on,

"If they come in their own boats, then you can charge five shillings for each person who enters The Castle. Later, if the interest is big enough, we might make it another shilling or even more."

For a moment the whole audience seemed to be stunned by what she had said.

Then one old man asked,

"Do you really think that people will come 'ere to see a Castle that's tumblin' down and a treasure they've never 'eard about before?"

"Of course they will come," Julia answered firmly. "I am quite certain that if the newspapers write about the treasure found in The Castle, a great number of our Clan will hurry to see it and there will obviously be historians and other writers who want to see for themselves what the Vikings longed to steal, but could not find."

There was silence for a moment and then one woman piped up,

"If we had the money to feed ourselves and our bairns, we would go down on our knees and thank you for bringin' us some hope for the future."

"That is what I want you to have," Julia said. "I promise you that I am not talking lightly. When I leave you now, I am going back to the ship I came to Scotland in."

She smiled at them all.

"Strange to relate it was only last night that the Captain, the previous owner of it, showed me the weapons of war he had collected in various parts of the world."

She could see that the people were edging forward with interest and she went on,

"They are just the sort of swords a Viking might have carried in his hand. They, if no one else, will cause a great deal of interest among historians."

"Will he really let us have them?" one man asked with disbelief in his voice.

"You will only be borrowing them," Julia said, "and, of course, you must return to everyone, when the excitement is over, all the items they have loaned you."

She hesitated before she added,

"But I am quite certain, and I want you to believe me, when I tell you that hidden treasure from the time of the Vikings discovered in an old Castle in Scotland will be thrilling news, which will attract a great number of people to this island and their money is just what is needed at this moment."

It was then that the women sitting on the ground with their children and the men standing round began to talk to each other in animated tones.

Their voices rose higher and higher, so it would have been impossible for Julia to make herself heard if she wanted to say anything further.

Instead she walked into The Castle and was glad when several men followed her.

She walked to what she thought was the centre of The Castle where there had once been a room with a proper floor and furniture.

But now if it had been made of wood it must have been collected for fires in the cottages.

There was just the rough earth with occasional tufts of grass coming through it.

She walked onto it and stood looking round to make sure that she was actually at the very centre of The Castle.

"Dig here!" she said. "I have a feeling that this is the place where they would have hidden their treasure. You must also make it impossible for anyone to enter The Castle except by the main door."

"You mean they'll sneak in without us knowin' to take the treasure from us?" a man asked.

"I cannot believe," Julia said, "that you do not have in your cottages something which was given to you through the ages."

She looked at them all expectantly.

"My mother used to tell me how the Scots like herself always treasure and keep what their ancestors had possessed which gave them a feeling of belonging to their own Clan."

"That be true," one man said. "My father 'ad several swords belongin' to me grandfather. I only sold 'em a month or so ago and I managed to give me bairns a decent meal with what I were paid for them."

"Try to get them back," Julia told him. "Look carefully in your houses and see if there is anything which would be of interest to those who will come not only to see the treasures you have discovered but also to write about them because they are a part of our history."

"Suppose they just laughs at us for tryin' to deceive 'em?" another man asked.

"I promise you they will not do that," Julia answered. "They will be so excited over the discovery that I am prepared to bet that in a few weeks, if not days, people will be coming to look at what you have found."

No one spoke and she then said almost sharply,

"Now get to work at once! Ask the women to collect everything they can find in the houses that still exist on the island and I will go back to where I am staying in Kildornock and bring you, not tomorrow but the next day, everything I have managed to beg, borrow or steal from those who will have no idea why I need them."

She emphasised the last words and there was no need for her to add, but she did,

"No word of what is happening must be heard outside this island until you have found and dug up the hiding place of your ancestors."

"Well, all I can say is that I may be a bit of a nut," one man said, "but I believe you. You can see what money means to us at the moment, and we 'ave nothin' to lose but everythin' to gain by doin' what you have just told us to do."

"Thank you very much," Julia replied. "That is exactly what I wanted you to say and now I would like to speak to the women again."

She walked out of The Castle to find, as she expected, that all the women were still where she had left them talking animatedly amongst themselves.

They were doubtless wondering if they could believe her and if her idea would bring in the sightseers she thought it would.

"I have found the place in The Castle," she said, "where the men can start digging at once. But what you have to find is everything that you can possibly find to fill it with the treasures your ancestors would have hidden away from all those terrifying Vikings."

"We ain't got much left," one woman said sharply.

"I know that," Julia answered. "But I have already told the men that I am going to bring a great number of things myself which I must borrow from friends, but which will be of interest to historians and other visitors I am sure that this island will engender in a very short time."

She paused for a moment.

Then she went on,

"But digging is hard work and just as your children are hungry, so are your husbands. Where do you buy your food when you have money to do so?"

"About half a mile down that road," one woman said, pointing her finger. "There be shops there that don't ask too much for what they sells us. But it's not often we can have anythin' I call real food."

She spoke bitterly and Julia said,

"I am going to give you one hundred pounds now to spend as wisely as you can and to buy substantial food like meat for the men who are working inside. I would also like you to buy some chocolate for the children."

"Chocolate!" one woman exclaimed. "That's not goin' to feed them as they ought to be fed."

"I know that," Julia agreed. "But because they have had so little to eat they will find real food difficult. Therefore, let them have some chocolate to start with. After that put them on something substantial."

"One hundred pounds will go a long way," one woman said, "but there be an awful lot of us."

"I do realise that," Julia told her. "And whoever goes shopping I want them to tell the man who keeps the shop that there will be another one hundred pounds worth of food to be collected tomorrow and the same amount again for a further two days."

She smiled at them all.

"I am reckoning that the men will have the hole in the ground ready by then and I will return the day after tomorrow with everything possible to add to what you have supplied from your own homes."

There was silence for a moment.

Then one of the women burst into tears.

"I don't believe this is happenin'," she said. "I'm sure I'm dreamin'. It's been like hell to see my bairns suffer. My mother died because we couldn't feed her properly. I'm sure I'm not hearin' you right."

She put her hands up to her eyes.

Julia walked to her and put her hand on her shoulder.

"It's true," she said, "and you have to believe me. I know that my mother, who is dead, sent me here to help you and it is God's idea, not mine, that you should find treasure. Even if it is not what it pretends to be, it will still be a means of bringing money to the island and food for your children."

It was then as if what Julia had said had been accepted and believed by the rest of the women.

Some of them were crying because the whole scenario was such a shock.

Others were wanting to shake Julia by the hand and tell her that they were sure that she had saved them.

"Now I must leave you," Julia said. "But here is the money for today's food."

She took out her purse as she spoke and gave the notes to the woman who had offered to do the shopping.

It was just as the Bank Manager had put it in and, as she had not had to spend anything while she was on board the yacht, she put the money into the woman's hand.

"I just don't believe it's real," she muttered, as the tears were running down her face.

She bent forward to kiss the money as if to make sure with her lips what she was seeing with her eyes.

"Now come with me," Julia said, "before I drive away you can travel with me in my carriage to the yacht. If you have too much to take back with you I am sure you will find someone to help."

"It's true! It's true!" the woman was saying over and over again. "This be real money and what I can buy with it will make us all feel different before we goes to bed."

"You will feel very different in the next few days," Julia told her. "Now I must hurry back to the yacht, so do come with me."

The woman slipped the money from her hand into a bag that one of the other women provided for her.

As Julia turned to walk round The Castle to where the boat she had come in was tied, they all followed her.

Some of them were cheering excitedly and the children ran beside her jumping for joy, although they did not know why everyone was so excited.

With the two women aboard the man rowed the boat back to the opposite side.

When they scrambled out, Julia told him that she owed him five shillings and would pay him tomorrow.

"This lady," she pointed out, "has all my money for the moment, but you will see me tomorrow and you can trust me as long as that."

"I'll trust you from here to Eternity if it all comes off as you said it will," the man answered.

"You were clever enough to think of one way to obtain money," Julia reminded him, "and now I have done the same. I think and I hope that you will soon find one boat is not enough to carry all the visitors and that is when you will need help."

"I wants to believe you," he replied.

"So do we all," the woman who was doing the shopping chimed in.

"I want to believe that I have said the right thing and done the right thing," Julia said. "It is something my mother, who was a MacCarn like you, would have approved of."

"I'm sure she'd have been ever so proud of you," the woman said. "You're only a wee girl, yet when you was talkin' to us, I thinks you might have been a man."

Julia realised that this was a compliment.

She merely thanked her as they had arrived at the shore where the boatman collected and returned his passengers. It was only a small bay and the land was not high above it.

All the same the path was rough and Julia thought that if many people walked on it in their effort to reach the island, it would have to be strengthened in some way or another.

However, she felt that she had made enough suggestions for one day.

She and the woman climbed into the carriage which was waiting for her while the boatman waved goodbye.

On Julia's instructions the woman told the driver where the shop was in the village.

Julia thought that he might protest at going further than he had intended but he good-humouredly accepted her directions and drove his horse as quickly as it would go.

It had obviously benefitted from its rest because they reached the village very swiftly.

There was a Kirk and then another street with just a few shops on either side of it and everything looked very down at heel.

None looked particularly inviting until at the end there was a much larger shop, which she saw at a glance sold almost everything that anyone would require.

She had told the people that she would give them money to spend for the next two days.

But when she was there she thought that she would be wiser to give the instructions herself.

She therefore left the woman who was eagerly spending the money that she had given her and asked to speak to the proprietor.

He was fetched from a nearby room and she saw that he was a Scotsman getting on in years. He gave the impression of being a man who understood his job and endeavoured to make the best of it.

Julia held out her hand to him and, as he took it, she said,

"I am the cousin of Mrs. Alistair MacCarn, who lived in this part of the world, but she is dead."

The proprietor did not answer, but she thought that he recognised the name and she went on,

"I am very upset to find that the people on the island are suffering from lack of food which very naturally means lack of money."

She looked around her for a brief moment and then continued,

"I have arranged with them that they should spend a hundred pounds a day with you for the next two days. After that I hope we will find some way of preventing them suffering in the future as they are at the moment."

The elderly man looked at her with surprise.

Then he said,

"Aye, things be bad for them as lives on the island. I thinks for some time that the Chieftain of the MacCarns should do something about it."

"I think that too," Julia agreed. "But because I have MacCarn blood from my mother, I am helping them. For the moment I am asking you to give them as much food for the money they have, as you can possible spare. Also food which is edible and good for people who appear to be emaciated and half-starved."

"That's the right word for it," he answered. "But we have our own troubles and our own difficulties and, although we are sorry for them, there seems to be nothing that we can do or suggest."

Julia thought that it would have been easy for him to let them have some food, but she thought it a mistake to say so at this particular time.

"All I ask," she replied, "is that you give them as much value as you can for the money I have given you and tomorrow there will be another sum for them to buy what is needed for the oldest man right down to the youngest of the appallingly thin children."

"I promise you, lady, I'll do my very best," the man told her.

She thought as he had not looked at her while he was speaking, he was somewhat ashamed that his neighbours should have suffered so badly.

She then said goodbye to the woman who was buying the food and told the coachman to take her back to the harbour as quickly as he could.

Because she was so anxious to move ahead with what she was planning, she found the hour that it took to reach the yacht infuriatingly long.

She wanted to call out with joy when she could see the houses of the village ahead and know that *The Mermaid* would be waiting for her.

Captain Wood was on the deck as she came aboard.

"I was wondering what had happened to you, my Lady," he said. "I thought you were just going for a drive and would be back for luncheon."

"I have had an adventure which I feel you will find hard to believe," Julia replied. "And to tell the truth, as I have had no luncheon, I am very hungry."

"Tea is now waiting for you," the Captain informed her, "and, as you have had no luncheon, I will tell the chef that you want something more substantial than cake."

Julia was ready to protest that she would wait for dinner, but already he had hurried away.

She went into the Saloon and sank down onto the soft sofa.

Then she pulled off her hat and threw it down beside her handbag.

The Captain came back and sat beside her.

"Now do tell me what you have been up to," he asked. "As you have been away such a long time I felt sure that you had found your relations, although I have learnt that they have moved South. It will therefore be impossible to find the cousin who you expected to be here."

Julia was hardly listening.

She was not really interested in herself at the moment, but the people of the island she was intending to help.

She told the Captain all that had happened from the time she had left him until she had given the shopkeeper in the village the money for the food.

The Captain listened intently and made no comment until she had finished.

Then he said,

"You are a very brave girl."

"I am brave in one way," Julia said, "and I am hoping and praying that you will lend the people, and I assure you they will be completely honest, some of the weapons you showed me last night which I know would be of great interest to any of the historians, who will undoubtedly come to the island as soon as they learn what treasures we have found there."

"From my collection?" the Captain questioned.

"I promise it will all be returned to you once everything is underway and you must tell me where I can find, or buy if I have to, ancient weapons or anything that the historians will believe are from the time of the Vikings."

The Captain looked at her.

Then unexpectedly he laughed.

"I cannot believe that this is true," he said. "You appear like an angel out of the sky and save your people. What I want to ask, and I am sure the same question is on your lips, is what on earth has happened to the Chieftain of the MacCarns that he is nowhere to be seen."

"That is just what I want to know," Julia replied, "but I expect, as I understand that his Castle is somewhere near here, that the local people will be able to tell us if he is at home or if they have any idea where he is."

"Are you going to tell him that he has neglected those who look to him for leadership?" the Captain asked.

"I will say something like that," Julia responded. "But I cannot believe that any man could ignore children who are little more than skin and bone."

She paused before she added,

"Therefore when they say they have not seen him for a long time, he must either have died or gone abroad."

"If he had died, I imagine they would have been told of it," the Captain said. "But, if he is abroad, then he will have every possible excuse for not looking after the people of his Clan properly."

"If I get the chance I will tell him that he should have put someone else in charge," Julia retorted. "How is it possible that a whole island of men, women and children should suffer as those I have just left are suffering?"

"Well, you have surely done what you can," the Captain replied, "and, of course, you shall have any of my collection of weapons which you think are suitable. At the same time I would like to have them back."

"That I promise you I will make them do," Julia told him. "And I would like you to come along and see the island for yourself."

"What would be a good idea," the Captain said, "is for me to take *The Mermaid* nearer to the island than we are at the moment."

"I had already thought of that," Julia remarked.

"I think we should ask a few questions in this village," the Captain went on, "as to what has happened to your relations. Then you might find well someone who would at least loan you something for the secret treasure, which you believe will attract a great number of visitors to the island."

Julia stared at him.

Then she said quickly,

"But that is impossible. If anyone local knows that we are collecting, they will put two and two together and guess that what is found on the island was not hidden there at the time of the Vikings' visits."

"I did not think of that," the Captain admitted. "Then I will have to be as generous as possible with my collection of weapons. I know that some of them are worth a great deal of money."

Julia had not been particularly interested when last night he had opened a door next to his cabin and shown her what she thought were rather ugly weapons stacked on every shelf and on the floor.

She had actually given them only a cursory glance and had then said,

"I am sure it must have been very interesting for you to make such a collection. But, as there are so many, I wonder if you will remember which country they came from?"

The Captain had laughed.

"I often ask myself that question. In fact the other day it took me several hours before I had remembered that the sword which was puzzling me had come from Sweden and I had found it in a dirty little shop which had no idea of its age or even of its value."

"That is how one can enjoy making a collection," Julia said. "I remember my mother finding it hard to resist jewels from countries when they went abroad. But she obtained some very ancient necklaces, which I will show you when I unpack my suitcase."

She was thinking as she spoke how glad she was that she had put them into her luggage and not left them to be found by her stepmother.

Her father had said,

"You will have to put them in the Picture Gallery and we must guard them very carefully when people go round in case they slip one into their pocket."

"Now you are scaring me," her mother had said. "So I will wear them to impress you, darling, and no one else, as far as I am concerned, is special enough to see them."

Her father had laughed.

"If I could only afford it, I would buy you diamonds, emeralds and sapphires from every country in the world. But, as it is, you will have to be content with my kisses and adoration of you."

"Which are more valuable to me than anything you can possibly buy," her mother had said.

Julia was playing with one of her dolls on the floor and they had forgotten her existence because they were so happy together.

Julia thought now that, if the worst came to the worst and her stepmother refused to let her have any money because she had run away, she would pawn the necklaces.

Then, when she could afford it, buy them back again.

After they had finished the delicious egg dish that the chef had cooked for them, the Captain said,

"I am not going to press you to have any more because I am sure that the chef is planning a special dinner for you. He will be disappointed if you don't eat every mouthful of it and love the different tastes."

Julia grinned and said that she would do her best.

But she could not help thinking that the people on the island would be having their first good meal for many weeks of nothing or very little.

She only hoped that the woman had been wise in her choice of food.

'Anyway the children will surely enjoy the chocolate,' she thought when she went to bed.

She was still thinking of them and praying that she had done the right thing until she fell asleep.

*

The next morning she woke up with a burning sense of excitement.

She had fallen asleep thinking of the islanders and woke wondering if they had spent a happy night.

Then she was aware that the yacht was moving and for a moment she thought that she must be dreaming.

Then, as she heard the waves splashing against the sides of *The Mermaid*, she jumped out of bed to look out of the porthole.

They were at sea, but travelling slowly along the side of the cliffs and above them she could see the moors.

It was very like the Captain, she thought, to take her as he had promised to the island and she thought that he would give them excellent advice, perhaps better than she had been able to do herself.

Without wasting any time she hurriedly dressed.

When she walked up to breakfast, she found the Captain waiting for her as she had expected in the Saloon.

"I had no idea you would leave so early," she said as she joined him.

"I knew that you would be wanting to get back to the island," he replied. "And I am becoming most curious to see it myself."

"I think the first thing we should do," Julia said, "is to see how far they have dug the hole for the hiding of the treasure, also what they have found to put in it from their own houses."

The Captain did not answer and she went on,

"We may be pleasantly surprised. Mama always said that the Scots hoarded the treasures of the past and very often complained that the present was not as exciting as it had been in their father's or grandfather's time."

"I don't suppose that it was particularly exciting to have the Vikings descending on you unexpectedly," the Captain said. "Unless the history books are wrong they very often killed the children, assaulted the prettiest girls or carried them away as prisoners and then stole everything that was valuable that they could find."

He paused for a moment before he added,

"I remember one place not so far from here where the Scots dug into a mountain and hid every member of their family the moment the Viking ships came into sight."

"If they did that, they would not have had time to hide their treasures," Julia said. "Therefore it is something you must not say. These people have to believe that their ancestors would have found a place in The Castle where they could hide what they wanted to keep and cherish in the future."

She spoke with such fierceness that the Captain smiled.

"I am not surprised you have convinced them that was what happened," he said. "I will therefore not be in the least surprised if when they are digging they find the original place where their treasures were hidden."

Julia gave a cry.

"Oh, if only they could do that, it would solve all their problems."

"As it is, you are waiting for me to solve yours," the Captain replied. "Well, as soon as we have had breakfast, we will go and look and see how far the diggers have got."

It was difficult for Julia not to leave at once because she was so eager to see if her instructions had been carried out by the locals.

But because it would be a mistake to upset the chef, she ate the excellent fish dish that he had cooked for them, also the French *crêpes* that he had conjured up so skilfully.

Then at last it seemed to her ages before *The Mermaid* came to a standstill.

When the yacht's landing boat was lowered, The Castle lay just ahead of them.

"At least I will not have to pay for this voyage," Julia said laughingly. "Nor will I have to swim if I cannot afford to pay for it."

The Captain smiled.

"You never know your luck, you may well have more surprises waiting for you than you anticipate."

"Now you are trying to frighten me," Julia said, "and I am sure that it will be as good if not better than I expect."

The landing boat carried them to the side of the island where it was easy to disembark.

As they then climbed up towards The Castle, Julia knew without him saying so, that the Captain was impressed by The Castle itself.

He was thinking, as she had thought, when she first saw it, how magnificent it must have been before it was destroyed and left in ruins.

As they had reached The Castle on the side of the island where there were no houses, they were not seen until they went round it.

Julia led the way to the front where she had spoken to the people and she saw that the Captain was looking down at the cottages and realised what a terrible state they were in, as well as The Castle.

Then, as she led him inside, she saw that there were two men so low in the ground that only their head and shoulders could be seen, while yet another three were looking down and encouraging them.

"Good morning," she called out.

They turned round and were obviously surprised to see her.

She walked up to the hole in the ground which they had made after she had left last night and obviously again early this morning.

"You have done splendidly," she said. "It must be four feet deep, if not more."

"It be hard work," one of the men said. "But we ain't found anythin' yet, but we hopes to do so with every spadeful we throws out."

"This is the Captain of *The Mermaid* which brought me from England," Julia told them. "As he is an expert on this sort of thing he will, of course, be able to answer any questions you may have."

"I really don't think there is any need for questions," the Captain said. "You have dug exceedingly well and very deep, which is exactly what your benefactor wanted."

"Do you think so?" one of the men asked. "Is she right in sayin' that so many people will come to the island to see the treasures hidden from them Vikings?"

"I am quite certain they will," the Captain replied. "I have brought some weapons that I myself have collected from around the world. But you must promise not to let anyone steal them and to give them back when your island is as prosperous as you want it to be."

"Of course," the man agreed. "We be Scottish and we don't steal, especially from those who helps us."

He spoke somewhat indignantly.

"That is just what I have told the Captain," Julia said. "They are, of course, very precious to him as he has been all round the world to collect them."

"I'd like to see them," one of the men said. "I've got my grandfather's sword, as we can put in the hole and me wife and I don't want to lose it."

"Of course not," Julia agreed, "and everything that is in the hole must be guarded carefully during the daytime and you must make it impossible for anyone to steal anything from here at night."

"That's what I says to Gordon," the man murmured.

"I think you have done a very good job," the Captain said before anyone else could speak. "But, if you will forgive me making this suggestion, I think that the hole should be a little wider."

He hesitated before he went on,

"If the Scots were running away from their enemies they would have thrown their treasure into it and the men would have covered up the hole immediately so that the place where it was hidden would have looked rough and not in any way attractive enough to command any attention."

The men thought this was good advice and started to enlarge the hole on both sides.

Then one of them piped up,

"I thinks I should thank you, miss, for the meal we 'ad last night. If you 'ad seen how happy it made everyone, you would have been really pleased."

"And the children," Julia asked, "did the children enjoy it?"

"The bairns enjoyed the chocolate and ate it as quick as they could. After that they went to bed real 'appy."

"That is what I wanted," Julia replied. "Now I wish to show the Captain your houses and after that perhaps your wives will bring up the treasures you are going to put into this hole as I don't think it need be any deeper."

She looked at the Captain as she spoke.

"It is deep enough now," he said, "because they would have to cover it if the Viking ships were on the horizon. If they had had to get away before they arrived, the hole would have to be filled up and not appear as a dip in the very centre of The Castle."

"We should all bring our goods here at twelve o'clock," Julia said. "Then someone can make a list of what is being put into the hole. You must all concentrate on making sure that no one can get into The Castle except through the main door and pay."

"We have done most of that already," one of the men said. "We thinks it's a mistake for anyone whose not one of us to see us workin' on it. So we've now covered up all what were windows on the ground floor and it'll be impossible and too dangerous for anyone to climb through them."

"You have done splendidly," Julia replied. "I think the sooner it all gets going the better."

"That's just what I were sayin' to young Angus," one man said. "If I lost me great-grandfather's medals he got when he were in the Army, I'd never hear the end of it."

"None of us must lose anything," Julia remarked. "We have to win and the more people who come to look at the hole the more food will be available for supper every evening and the children will soon grow as tall as their fathers."

"I only hopes you tells us the truth," one man muttered beneath his breath.

"I am sure you will be able to see in two weeks' time that I have been right," Julia said confidently. "And if I could afford to bet I would most certainly bet on it."

The man laughed.

They were all in a good humour when Julia went down to the village with the Captain.

She asked them all to bring anything they had to lend to The Castle at noon.

As they greeted her with smiles because she was helping them, Julia found it easy to forget the dilapidated condition of their houses.

Worst of all was the emptiness for the occupants inside, as some of the cottages only had a table and two chairs and nothing else.

When she peeped into a bedroom, she saw that the bed itself had been sold and the man and his wife were sleeping on the floor.

'How can things have been allowed to get so bad?' she asked herself again.

At twelve o'clock it was amazing that everyone on the island brought something to put in the hiding place in the centre of The Castle.

There were medals and little bits of jewellery, most of it in such a bad state that they could not sell it.

There was an ancient gun which had been broken and beyond repair besides several swords and some other strange implements, which had been used perhaps three hundred years ago by a builder.

When the Captain drew from a box the items he was giving, there was first a gasp from the people watching.

Then, when he pushed them into the hole, they cheered him. They were certainly worth having as treasures as Julia well knew.

As they had all been collected from different countries, they were, each of them, different in themselves.

Some of them were ornamented with strange stones and one sword that came from as far away as Japan boasted a mosaic of bright colours.

The women and children clapped enthusiastically.

"Now when you have done exactly what I asked," Julia said, "I must tell you how proud I am of the splendid and quick way you have agreed to my suggestions."

She smiled before she went on,

"I am going to write to all the newspapers in Scotland telling them what we have found. Also to tell the people in the villages what has happened here."

She looked round at their attentive faces.

"All of them will be enormously surprised at what we have discovered," she continued, "and it just happened when one of the men was taking away a beam which had fallen from the very top of The Castle. He saw that the ground was soft and dug there out of sheer curiosity."

She paused for breath before she carried on,

"To his amazement he saw that there was an instrument of some sort under the sand and dug a little further. That is the story and we must all keep to the same one."

Everyone listening nodded their heads in agreement and she added,

"God bless you all. I know that this has been a turning point in your lives and you are all going to benefit from what will happen as soon as the story comes out that a wonderful treasure has been found in the ancient Castle."

They clapped Julia when she had finished speaking.

Then one of the men said,

"Don't worry, we'll not let you down and we'll pray it'll happen as you says it will."

I am sure it will," Julia replied.

She climbed into the landing boat, which took her with the Captain back to *The Mermaid*.

They waved until they reached the yacht.

"So what are you going to do next?" the Captain then asked her.

"I will sit down to write a number of letters," she replied to him. "Then I want someone to post them as soon as I have addressed them. I would be very grateful if you could find, as I am sure you can, any old newspapers aboard which will have the address of where the newspaper is published."

"I will do that for you," the Captain promised. "And, as you suggest, we will move a little further along the coast. There is a fairly large town about two miles from here and that would be the place to post your letters and also to tell the people while you are doing so what amazing things you have discovered on the island."

"That is a good idea," Julia cried. "I will start writing the letters immediately. I hope you have some notepaper which is not printed, as I think it must be an anonymous reader to the newspaper in question who thinks that the Editor would like to hear of this new discovery."

The Captain smiled.

"You really think of everything," he said. "In fact I am beginning to think that you are too clever to be a woman and you ought to have been born a man!"

"That is a compliment I do appreciate," Julia laughed. "But I assure you that my two brothers are going to be much cleverer than I have ever been."

As the Captain was determined to have the last word, he said,

"They will doubtless end up either as the Prime Minister or a Member of the Royal Family!"

Julia grinned.

"I only hope you are right. In the meantime, woman or not, I have to help those people on that dilapidated and unhappy island."

CHAPTER SIX

Julia wrote her letters and was surprised at the number of newspapers that were in circulation in Scotland.

Some of them were weekly magazines that she thought would be just as interested in her story as the daily newspapers should be.

By the time she had finished, *The Mermaid* had moved out to sea and was rocked by the waves as the Captain made for the town.

However, he brought *The Mermaid* into a quiet bay just before he reached it.

"We shall stay here for the night," he said. "I don't think we will be disturbed. The Scots may be very keen on going by boat, but in my own experience they never have been very good swimmers!"

Julia laughed.

At the same time she was thinking that the people on the island would not be strong enough to swim against the waves and, if the children attempted to do so, they would undoubtedly have risked being drowned.

She found it difficult to think or talk of anything but the people on the island.

It was then that the Captain said,

"You are not to worry yourself too much about them. After all you are a stranger to these parts and they have lived here long enough for their elders to have fought for them and saved them from the terrible conditions they are now in."

"But they are *my* people," Julia answered. "I have the blood of the MacCarns in me and I would feel exactly the same if my brothers were treated in the same manner."

"I expect they will soon be old enough to come North and fish for salmon in the rivers and shoot the grouse on the moors in the way the Scotsmen traditionally enjoy themselves," the Captain commented.

Julia knew that he was trying to cheer her up and he smiled at her.

"Your letters have all gone out," he said, "and I think I will walk down to the town and if I see anyone sensible like a Bank Manager or perhaps a Clergyman I will tell them about the treasure that has been found on the island."

"Oh, please do that!" Julia said. "The sooner people get there, even if it is only a few sightseers, the more it will thrill those who have given up everything they regard as precious and placed them in The Castle."

"Just as I have done," the Captain replied. "I should be very annoyed if one of the visitors steals something that I have brought all the way from China or Japan. Therefore, I will never see it again."

"I am sure that will not happen," Julia answered. "I told them that someone must always be on duty. Not only to protect the treasures in the centre of the Castle but also to be certain that they pay their way."

"You are quite right," the Captain agreed. "They should certainly do that. I will feel disappointed if they did not make a lot of money out of the precious objects which were supposedly hidden from the Vikings."

When Julia went to bed that night, she prayed for a long time that her idea of saving the people on the island would be successful.

'There are not really a great number of them,' she said to herself, "but then the children will suffer perhaps more than anyone and I could never forgive the Chieftain for neglecting them so disgracefully.'

When she did fall asleep, she had a dream that she was running across the heather to save the weapons she held in her hand and was being pursued by a horde of Vikings who were following her.

*

When she awoke, she laughed at herself for being so stupid.

At the same time, as it had really happened, she knew that many of the women and the men had run for safety to the hills where they would hide themselves until the Vikings left for home.

After she had finished breakfast, she realised that *The Mermaid* was moving and asked if they were going back to The Castle.

"Although you may well be angry with me," the Captain said, "I have now taken you in the opposite direction. I think it would be a mistake for you to sit around hoping that your first customer will arrive."

He smiled at her as he continued,

"You will be disappointed if, as your letters have only just reached the newspapers this morning, no one will be there investigating the island until tomorrow."

Julia knew that he was thinking of her and what he said was indeed sensible.

Equally she so longed to be back on the island again, simply because she felt that there must be something more they could do to The Castle.

She only hoped that the men would have carried out her instructions and made it impossible for anyone to enter, except through the main door.

"You have come here to Scotland to see the view," the Captain said, "and I would like you to go on the bridge and watch where we are going from there."

Because she had nothing else to do, Julia immediately went to the bridge and found it an excellent place from which to admire the land they were passing.

The Captain kept *The Mermaid* near to the shore and Julia had a good view of the moors and some smaller villages as they sailed by.

Then, as they passed some particularly spectacular land, they entered a large bay in the middle of which was another Castle.

It was larger and far more beautiful than any Julia had seen before.

As it was built high above the sea, it seemed to tower over the garden where there was a mass of flowers and trees in blossom.

The Castle itself had a tall Tower in the centre of it with a pointed turret on each side.

The sun was shining on the windows and Julia thought that it was the most beautiful Castle she had ever seen.

It would be impossible to live in such a perfect place and not be happy.

At the same time the question was in her mind as to why the inhabitants of The Castle had not been aware of the suffering further North of the MacCarn Clan whose Castle was so ruined and dilapidated.

"I wonder who lives there?" she asked the Captain.

"It is surely one of the finest castles I have ever seen," he answered, "and I am certain that if the owner has a yacht like *The Mermaid* it could rest in comfort in that quiet bay."

They sailed on a little further.

Then, after they had had luncheon, the Captain said that he would take her back.

"I cannot allow you," he said, "to visit your pet Castle tonight because you will be so upset if no one has actually visited it."

Julia gave a sudden cry.

"I have just remembered now that I forgot to send the hundred pounds I promised for food to the shop in the village. Oh, dear, do you think he might allow them to have anything if they don't have the money to pay for it?"

"Because I have swept you away against your will," the Captain said, "I sent the money before we moved on. So your people will have had luncheon, tea and I hope dinner before you go to bed."

"Oh, how kind of you!" Julia replied. "It was so stupid of me to forget, but, when you said you were taking me away, I kept worrying about them instead of enjoying, as I should have done, the way that *The Mermaid* was sweeping serenely through the rough waves."

"*The Mermaid* has been in worse seas than this," the Captain told her.

"She is such a lovely yacht," Julia said, "I cannot think how you could bear to part with her. But Hubert told me that he had bought it from you."

"I will let you into a little secret," the Captain replied. "I built myself another *Mermaid*, which is superior to this one and has all the latest engines and can, in fact, move at twice the speed of this one."

"So that is why you were selling her," Julia said.

"She went for fifteen years," the Captain explained, "but I had a great passion for moving quicker and having all the latest innovations which have been invented since *The Mermaid* was first finished."

"I am sure she will miss you," Julia replied. "Although I feel certain that Hubert will enjoy taking her to many parts of the world, she will still miss you."

"The trouble with you," the Captain said, "is that you are always thinking of other people instead of yourself. I am selfish enough to want the very best, the newest and something different. You will always be kind and loving to those who have served you and that is exactly how a woman should be."

Julia laughed.

"That is a beautiful compliment and, as I have not had many in my life, I will most certainly treasure it."

"I am sure you will find that there are a great number of men who will pay you compliments," the Captain said. "But promise me now that you will not marry until you are really in love."

Julia had already told him that she had run away from home because her stepmother had wanted her to marry a man she did not love and who did not love her.

She had not told him who it was, but, as they lived close to each other, in fact their estates joined, she had told Hubert that she wanted to escape and that was why he had sent her to *The Mermaid*.

"You were very wise," the Captain said, "and I am sure that your mother, who you told me was happy with your father, would want you to marry only if you were really in love with the man who was in love with you."

Julia sighed.

"That is what I think everyone wants. But we are not always lucky enough to find what we are seeking."

"I am not a clairvoyant," he replied, "but I promise you with your pretty face and your kind and warm heart, that you will find the right man one of these days and the right man will find you."

"I only hope that your prediction will come true," Julia answered, "and promise me that you and *The Mermaid* will not sail too far away into the sunset and you will be able to come to my Wedding."

"I will most certainly," the Captain replied. "My present will be a sword from some outlandish place you have never seen before!"

Julia chuckled.

She did not protest when he took *The Mermaid* into the quiet bay where they had been the night before.

He made it quite clear that he did not expect her to go, as she wanted to, to see if The Castle was still there and find out if anyone had come to visit it.

*

Julia slept peacefully.

But when she awoke and found that the sun was pouring in through the portholes, she thought, with a leap of her heart, that today would be significant.

'Nothing and no one will stop me going to The Castle, as soon as I have had breakfast,' she determined.

She dressed herself quickly and went into the Saloon to find that the Captain was already there and her breakfast was waiting for her.

"I know what you are going to say to me," he said, "and a boat and two oarsmen are waiting for you as soon as you have finished your breakfast."

"You are kind," Julia murmured, "and you do spoil me. But you know how anxious I am just in case something goes wrong."

She paused before she added,

"Perhaps the letters have not reached the newspapers or the people in the village have not talked as we wanted them to do."

The Captain did not reply.

And after a moment she continued,

"There are certain to be a crowd of visitors to this part of Scotland at this time of the year and even the salmon fishing must be prepared to wait while the treasure in The Castle attracts the fishermen!"

"I doubt if anything attracts sportsmen like sport," the Captain remarked, somewhat dryly. "But I am not prepared to argue with you and I am sure that those who live on the island are wondering how soon they will see you again."

"That is what I hope they will think," Julia said.

She finished breakfast and the Captain said, as she put down her cup of coffee,

"Now be off with you! I will come to collect you about luncheon time because even the most ardent enthusiast has to eat. Then if you would wish to return, *The Mermaid* is at your service."

"You do spoil me and I love you for it," Julia told him. "Thank you! Thank you for being so understanding. But I find it impossible to think of anything but our Treasure Island, as we might just as well call it."

She did not wait for the Captain to answer, but ran to the side of *The Mermaid* and climbed into the landing boat which was waiting for her.

The two oarsmen rowed her out into the sea and they moved swiftly towards the island.

Looking at it in the same dilapidated state as it had been before, Julia decided that she would somehow like to obtain a flag, which should be put on the very top of it, so that it blew out triumphantly in the wind.

'It will be welcome to those who are curious about The Castle,' she told herself. 'It will certainly look more attractive than it does at the moment.'

In fact, as she drew nearer, she thought that The Castle looked even more destroyed and crumbling than it had seemed yesterday.

Then she laughed at herself for expecting miracles to happen and The Castle to become as beautiful as the one they had seen further down the coast.

There were two empty boats at what had always been the entrance to The Castle.

As she climbed up to the land, she saw two men and then realised that one of them was the man who had first taken her to the island.

They smiled when they saw her.

But before they could speak she asked,

"Have you brought anyone here?"

"You'll see that for yourself when you goes inside," one of the men replied. "This be the third journey I've made this mornin'."

Julia gave a cry of joy.

Without waiting to hear more of what they had to say she ran towards The Castle.

As she turned round at the main door which faced the village beneath it, she saw that a good number of well-dressed holiday-makers were coming out of The Castle.

One woman was holding the hand of a little girl and another had a boy who was obviously older.

They were coming back to the boats to be taken to the shore.

She then entered The Castle and found just inside the door there was one of the women, who was taking the money the visitors paid to enter.

"Oh, it be you, miss!" she said when she saw Julia. "I thinks for a moment you be one of the visitors. You know you haven't got to pay!"

Julia saw that there were several people in the centre of The Castle grouping round the discovered treasure.

"Have they been interested in what they have seen?" she asked in a whisper.

"They be just thrilled to bits," the woman replied. "We've taken thirty-one shillings already this mornin' and we had six visitors last night who all paid up their five shillings, so we be feelin' rich."

Julia smiled at her.

She knew from the enthusiastic note in her voice that the woman was as excited as she was herself.

There was now a growing murmur from the voices of the visitors round the treasure.

Then three well-dressed people with two children came walking towards the door.

"Well, I think it's a real miracle," one was saying, "that they should find these precious things after all these years. You would have thought that someone might have gone on digging before now, just in case something was hidden when the poor creatures had to run away from the deadly Vikings."

Julia did not wait to hear the answer.

She moved towards the centre of the Castle and found in charge that there was one of the men who had dug the hole in the first place.

"It be just as you thought, miss," he said to Julia before she could speak. "They comes here and goes away thrilled and so excited that such a treasure should have been hidden in the ground for so long."

"I am so glad! So very glad!" Julia answered him.

"As you see we has made it impossible to get into The Castle except through the main door and everyone has paid up and made no fuss about it."

"That is just what I hoped would happen," Julia said.

Then, as she heard voices behind her, she turned round to see that several more people were arriving.

Because it was so fascinating she moved into the back of The Castle.

She sat watching the people paying their way at the door and coming in to stare at the treasures.

The man who was in charge turned them over to please each visitor and in many cases, she then realised, he was giving a very untruthful story of what the weapon was and how it was supposed to function.

But as long as they were told where it had come from, it did not seem to matter.

He was wise enough not only to show them the many weapons, most of which had come from the Captain, but some of the pieces that had been lent by the people in the village.

Also the many necklaces that Julia hoped would not be damaged in any way because they obviously meant so much to the owners.

"How deep does the hole go?" one man asked.

It was a question that was repeated by quite a number of visitors.

The answer, however, was exactly what Julia wanted and was indecisive.

"There might be a great deal more lower down," the man in charge replied. "Or there might be other hidin' places anywhere round us, but we only found this one by chance and we'll have to do a great deal more diggin' to see if there be any more."

"I hope that is true," more than one visitor said. "We'll come back next year to see if you have found more surprises for us."

Two more boatloads came during the morning.

Then the Captain appeared to insist that Julia came back to *The Mermaid* for her luncheon.

"It's so exciting," she enthused, "do stay with me this afternoon and listen to what they say. I was right! I was right! They were all thrilled as you said they would be. Now they are quite certain that there are other hiding places we have not yet discovered."

The Captain laughed.

"You will have to start collecting again," he said. "I have no more to lend you and I don't suppose that there is a house in the village that has any treasure they have not already put into that hole."

"They are so pleased," she replied. "Two of the women came to me with tears in their eyes and said that God would bless me because they would all be able to have a decent meal for the first time for years."

Because their gratitude had been so moving, she felt the tears come into her own eyes again.

Tactfully the Captain began to talk of other things.

Nevertheless she hurried through luncheon and insisted on going back to The Castle long before the Captain wanted her to do so.

When she returned to The Castle, she was not surprised to find that there was only one man there.

The women who had taken the money had gone to enjoy all the food that had been bought from the shop in the other village.

"You go now and have your luncheon," Julia said to him, "and I will look after The Castle for you. Any visitors who will be coming here this afternoon will at the moment be eating luncheon and wondering what they would do if they themselves discovered treasure hidden from the Vikings."

The man laughed.

"That is what they wonder. If you asks me, the Vikings had no brains in their heads, as you has, and took everythin' they could carry with them and that weren't much!"

"Don't think about it," Julia said. "It frightens me. Go and enjoy your luncheon and I will see that everyone pays and no one steals anything."

The man laughed again, but hurried away to the village where the chimneys were smoking.

Julia was certain that the wives were cooking a delicious meal from food that had been delivered from the shop.

The earth which had been dug out of the ground had been thrown casually near to the hole where the treasure had been placed.

In order to disguise it from what it really was, it had been covered with a piece of tarpaulin.

On top of that were some small broken beams, which were not too uncomfortable to sit on.

Julia knew that it was unlikely that anyone would come to the door in the next hour or so.

She therefore made herself comfortable.

She could see some of the Captain's strange weapons from where she was sitting.

She was trying to guess from which country they had come, when a voice startled her by booming out,

"What is going on here?"

She looked up from the treasure and saw that, standing near her with his back to the front door, was a tall good-looking young man.

He was very well dressed in his kilt of the MacCarn tartan.

He was, she thought, younger and smarter than anyone she had seen since she had arrived in Scotland.

"I am sorry," she said apologetically, "I did not hear you arrive. I should have been at the door taking the entrance fee, which is five shillings."

"So I believe," the Scotsman replied. "I hear that there is a treasure, which has just been discovered."

"It is right there in the centre of The Castle," Julia said, pointing with her hand. "It must have been put there when the poor people who lived here in the past were trying to escape from the Vikings."

"I find it extraordinary that I have not heard of any of this before," he commented. "In fact I rather suspect that it is not genuine."

Julia gave a cry of horror.

"You have no right to say that!" she retorted. "Who are you?"

The man looked at her.

Then he replied in a somewhat quieter tone,

"I am the Duke of MacCarn-Drummond or indeed to put it another way the Chieftain of the MacCarns."

Julia gave a gasp.

Then she said,

"You are just the person I have been wanting to meet. I am horrified and ashamed that the Chieftain of any Clan could possibly allow his people to suffer as these poor people on the island have suffered."

She paused for breath before she added,

"As a MacCarn myself, I cannot believe that you were aware of how much they were suffering and actually starving to death."

The handsome Scotsman stared at her.

"So why are you saying all this to me?" he asked her sharply.

"Because if you are the Chieftain of our Clan," Julia expostulated, "someone must have told you how these people are hurting. Come, let me show you something."

She walked towards the entrance.

Outside, looking down at the village, she pointed at the broken roofs and the smashed windows.

The man beside her did not speak.

Then the door of one of the houses quite near to them opened and three children came out.

They were going out to play games on the ground which surrounded The Castle that was the only piece of grass covered land in the village.

They were all three appallingly dressed with torn and dirty clothes.

And because they were so emaciated, they moved very slowly.

One of them was dragging her feet as if walking on the rough ground was painful.

"Look at those children!" Julia exclaimed. "Just look at them! Luckily they are more active than some of the children who may be dead already. They were dying, as their parents are, by starvation. Yet you, as Chieftain of their Clan, did nothing about it."

The Duke did not speak for a moment.

Then he said,

"I had no idea. No idea at all that things were as bad as this."

"Then you should have known," Julia answered. "I just cannot understand how all this misery could have gone on, year after year, and you just let it happen."

She drew in her breath before she continued,

"The death toll of the older people is horrifying. There is no doubt that many of those who are alive will not live long. But it is the children who are suffering the most or were until yesterday when the first visitors came to inspect the treasure in The Castle and paid to go in."

"I cannot understand why I was not told about this," the Duke replied.

"Someone must have told you," Julia came back at him. "As the Chieftain of the Clan, it is your *duty* to help them."

"I am aware of that," the Duke answered sharply. "But as it happened I was abroad with my Regiment in India. I only returned to Scotland a few days ago."

Julia drew in her breath.

"Oh," she said, "I did not know that. I am sorry if what I said was very rude, but I have been so upset by what I found, I had to do something to save them."

"So then it was your idea," the Duke replied, "to find a hidden treasure in The Castle."

She looked round as if someone might be listening to their conversation.

"You must not say that," she whispered. "I want the people, especially the newspapers, to believe that the treasure is genuine and really was hidden by the MacCarns, who were, as you well know, continually invaded by aggressive marauding Vikings many centuries ago."

"I did know that they invaded this part of Scotland," the Duke said. "In fact they not only killed men and children and carried away the women but also stole everything they possibly could."

"I have read about it in history books," Julia answered quickly. "That is why I persuaded the men here to dig this hole and send out the message, which you have doubtless heard, that in doing so they found the treasures that the local people hid before they ran for safety to the high ground."

"I have read that too," the Duke told her. "But I had no idea, and you must believe me when I tell you this, that my people are suffering."

He smiled at her.

"As I have already said," he went on, "I was in India with my Regiment and, when my father died in Edinburgh after a long illness, it was three months before I could get away. I only reached England a fortnight ago."

There was no doubt from what he had just said that he was telling the truth as well as apologising.

"I am sorry," Julia said, "if I was rude. But it upset me, when I came here three days ago, to see the terrible way that the children were suffering. I learnt that, as they had no money, they were all in a state of near-starvation."

"So what did you do?" the Duke asked Julia.

"I gave them one hundred pounds a day for food and this is the third day. The people I have seen already appear to be looking better. But as you see the children are still very weak and not playing as children should, simply because they do not have the strength to do so."

She pointed as she spoke to the children beneath them who were sitting on the ground.

One of them was kicking at a ball with his foot, but they were making no effort to play with it as children would usually do.

"Now I understand what you have done," the Duke said, "I can only thank you from the bottom of my heart and promise you that this will never happen again."

"That is exactly what I wanted you to say," Julia cried. "Once things are normal, which will undoubtedly take time, you must think of something else that they can do to make money, because the people, who have loaned the treasures which were hidden inside The Castle, will want them back."

The Duke laughed.

"I am sure that they will. In the meantime, I have a great number of treasures which can be added. Incidentally it was one of the newspaper reporters who told me that the treasure had been discovered. I suppose that too was your doing?"

"I wrote to every Scottish newspaper I knew the name of," Julia informed him, "and all the magazines as well that are published in Edinburgh and Glasgow."

She could not help giving a little cry of delight as she added,

"The visitors have been pouring in the men told me when I arrived here this morning and I have only been left in charge while they enjoy a good meal, which they have not had for years."

"You are making me feel more awful than I do already," the Duke said. "But I was very sure when I was in India that my father would have left someone in charge who would look after the people of the Clan as he had always done when he was well enough."

"So what happened to this man?" Julia asked.

"I only heard yesterday, after I had been told that this treasure had been found here, that he died four years ago and had never been replaced. You cannot blame my mother, who was looking after my father in Edinburgh where he was in a hospital. Nor the other members of my family who, like myself, were abroad."

"We had no idea that this was happening," Julia said. "At the same time surely there was someone in the Clan who would look after those who were suffering as much as all these people were."

The Duke made a gesture with his hands.

"I think that the Clan is rather short of those who are rich enough to care for the very poor. As we are in the very far North of Scotland, many of the people in the last few years have moved further South."

He smiled at her.

"In fact the Clan just here is very small," he continued, "and not of great consequence. I can only imagine that no one went out of their way to enquire about all those who were less fortunate than they were."

Julia felt that there was nothing else she could say.

There was then silence until the Duke asked,

"How then are you a MacCarn and where do you come from?"

"I am visiting Scotland for the first time," Julia told him. "I wanted to find my mother's cousin, but she has left her house and no one in the village knows exactly where she might have gone."

"I can tell you that," the Duke answered her. "She is in Edinburgh or she was a month ago. Now I think of it, I did hear that she was thinking of moving a little further South."

Julia sighed.

"Then I will be sorry not to see her. At the same time it is not a great problem for me."

The Duke was silent for a moment.

And then he said,

"I think, if I am not mistaken, you must be travelling in the very smart yacht I passed as I came to the village."

"You are quite right," Julia said. "But it is not mine. It was only lent to me by a friend, because the Captain was going to Scotland."

She smiled at him.

"I had no idea, of course, that I would find anything as upsetting," she continued, "and as terrible as the MacCarns are suffering here. But I do think that they will acquire quite a lot of money, which they desperately need, from the visitors to The Castle."

"I can only say that it was a brilliant idea of yours," the Duke said. "What I would like to suggest now is that you come with me to my Castle and find among the treasures there, and there are plenty of them, items that will keep the visitors talking and delight those who are reporting the amazing finds in the newspapers."

Julia looked up at him with excited eyes.

"Can we really do that?" she asked. "I have one lot of really good old weapons that the Captain of the yacht has lent me. But the rest are not all that impressive and what I think we need more than anything else are the sort of things that a woman would hide because she did not want to lose them."

The Duke smiled.

"And in other words, jewels," he said. "Well, there are plenty of them at Carn Castle and you can choose anything you like."

"That is very generous of you and I can only say thank you on behalf of your people!" Julia replied without a trace of sarcasm.

She went to the side of The Castle and looked down the cliff.

Then she came back to say,

"I have a distinct feeling that more people are arriving and I think that the men and women who were in charge here will soon be back at their posts."

She glanced down again at the village and exclaimed,

"Oh, here they come! Unless you want to talk to them and also to the visitors, I think we should move away as quickly as possible."

"I agree with you," the Duke answered, "and I always was a very bad liar. I should be terrified of putting my foot in it, as you might say."

Julia laughed.

"You must not do that!" she urged him. "Everyone must believe that this really is the treasure that was hidden from the Vikings and I can assure you that they find it very exciting and what they want to believe."

At that moment the woman in charge and the other man, both rather breathless from hurrying up the side of the hill, came face to face with them.

"I'm sorry we've been so long," the woman said, "but my husband said it was the best meal he'd had for over two years and he wasn't goin' to miss a single crumb of it."

"I felt the same," the man behind her said. "I want to thank you from the bottom of my heart for feedin' me when I least expected it."

"Well, you can expect even more tomorrow," Julia said, "because a boatload of visitors has just arrived!"

The woman gave a cry and ran off to her place by the door.

The man, who had been looking curiously at the Duke, hurried in to stand by the secret hiding place.

The people walking up towards The Castle were typical sightseers.

Two women who were very well-dressed and obviously came, Julia thought, from a suburban town.

And two men, who Julia assumed were their husbands, appeared to be Bank clerks or shopkeepers.

One of the couples had a pretty little girl with them, who was saying plaintively,

"I have left my doll in the boat. I do so hope she will be safe."

"I am sure she will be safe, my dear," her mother said. "Now come along and see what excitement there is inside this big Castle."

They appeared not to notice Julia and the Duke, who stood to one side.

They paid the woman at the door, then hurried to look at the treasure in the centre of The Castle.

The Duke and Julia then slipped out the way they had come.

As they went down towards his rowboat, he commented,

"That is another two pounds ten shillings for you unless the children are half price."

"I suggested that they should be if they were old enough to come in, but those who are in a pram can stay outside in the sunshine."

The Duke laughed.

"You have thought of everything. I think that Heaven must have sent you to us to save our people and also to make them think for themselves. Surely someone before now could have managed to find some way of making money here rather than starving."

"I think that the land round here is owned by the Duke," Julia said, "and from what I heard one man say he required no extra workmen on his estate."

"That is something I can change now I have returned," the Duke replied.

They got into the Duke's rowboat, which was rowed by two well-dressed oarsmen.

They did not speak as they then moved off from the shore.

As Julia had already anticipated she found the Duke's Castle was indeed the beautiful one she had seen on the previous day with the Captain.

As they rowed swiftly towards it, she then turned to the Duke and said,

"I saw this Castle yesterday and thought that it was the most beautiful one I have ever seen. How could you be so lucky as to possess anything quite so magnificent?"

"I have often thought that myself," the Duke answered. "I loved living here as a small boy. But I was sent to a school in Edinburgh before going on to Oxford University. After that I joined the Scots Guards and, as I have just told you, was sent out to India where I have been for almost three years.

"Did you miss Scotland for all those years?" Julia asked him.

"I suppose being a Scot I missed it more than I can put into words," the Duke admitted. "But now that I am here and can enjoy every moment, I promise you that there will not be a member of the Clan who will not be looked after and found some sort of work that he is capable of doing."

"As you own so much land here and, as Scotland is as beautiful as I had expected it to be," Julia remarked, "I cannot believe that there should be any suffering in the Kingdom over which you reign."

"I can only promise you that I will make sure that the sort of dreadful situation you have just discovered will never happen again in the future," the Duke answered.

She thought, although she had hated him at first for what had happened, that it would be wrong of her to go on accusing him of it when it was really and truly not his fault.

Then, as the rowboat came to a stop beside the jetty, the Duke sprang out and put out his hand.

"Now come and see my Castle that I am so very proud of," he said, "and I would like you to appreciate it too as you are a member of my Clan."

As Julia took his hand, she felt a strange vibration run through her body.

This was really something that she had not expected, yet it had happened and she could hardly believe it.

"I am so longing to see – your Castle," she managed to stammer.

As they walked, side by side, through the flower garden beneath The Castle walls, she thought, jumping from one place to another, it was like a fascinating story which was something that she had never expected to happen in real life.

Yet it was and, as she walked up the stone steps, which led to The Duke's Castle, she thought that she had never known anything so wonderful or so exciting as what was happening to her at this moment.

CHAPTER SEVEN

The rooms inside The Castle were as beautiful as Julia had expected them to be.

As her father owned such fine furniture and pictures, she could recognise the work of famous artists as soon as she saw them.

And she was seldom wrong in pricing antique furniture especially when much came from France.

As they went from room to room, the Duke explained to her what each one was normally used for and Julia recognised most of the different contents.

Equally she was aware that the Duke had studied, as she had, the differing developments of painters and craftsmen over the centuries.

Finally, they came to a sitting room where an old lady with white hair was reclining on a sofa.

"Don't move, Aunt Elsie," the Duke suggested. "I have brought someone to meet you, who is as appreciative as you are, of the contents of this Castle. In fact she knows a great deal about art."

Aunt Elsie smiled and held out her hand to Julia, who took it in hers.

"I was an artist myself a long time ago," she said, "but unfortunately my eyes prevent me now from seeing even half of the beautiful objects in this Castle."

"I have never seen such a marvellous collection!" Julia enthused.

She thought that she was being somewhat unfair to her father by saying that he was an exception to her rule.

But she thought it a mistake to say to strangers who she was, just in case for no particular reason her stepmother learnt where she was and to all intents and purposes in hiding.

She might insist on her returning immediately.

Then once again she would be fighting to save herself from being married to some strange man she did not love and who certainly was not in love with her.

Instead, when the Duke said that he had another room to show her, she responded eagerly that she was anxious to see it as well.

They then said 'goodbye' to his aunt and went out of the room closing the door.

"I thought it important," the Duke said, "not to waste much time in taking the things I am giving to The Castle. That will then release the weapons that belong to the Captain of your yacht."

"It is essential," Julia replied, "that the newspapers, if they come in answer to my letter, should not describe the wrong treasures that are in The Castle and it is only reasonable that the best pieces should belong to the Chieftain of the Clan."

She paused for a moment before she added,

"After all I assume your ancestors before you were all Chieftains of the MacCarns."

"They were indeed," the Duke answered. "In fact the Clan goes back in time to the very early days of Scottish history. We are very proud of being one of the first, as well as one of the largest Clans, that has ever been written about by historians of Scotland."

"I thought we must have a reason for giving ourselves airs," Julia remarked and the Duke laughed.

"In Scotland we always take ourselves very seriously," he replied. "You must not laugh at my importance, otherwise I will reprimand you most firmly."

She was about to answer him when he added,

"Just as you reprimanded me and it is something I will never forget!"

"Oh, but you must," Julia said. "How was I to know that you were in India and therefore not responsible for what was happening at home? But I do think that one of your family should have remembered that the Clan is often in trouble and someone should have reported the situation to you, wherever you might be."

"And, of course, I would have done something about it," the Duke pointed out.

He paused before he carried on,

"Well, it is too late now to look back. What we have to do is to look forward. I promise you that as soon as we have chosen what you want to put in the special hiding place in The Castle, I intend to give orders that until everyone on the island is in good health, food of every sort will be delivered day by day to them."

"That is what I have arranged for them now," Julia said.

"It is something I cannot allow you to give for more than today and perhaps tomorrow," the Duke replied.

He thought that Julia was going to argue with him and said,

"After all, you have told me that I am your Chieftain and you have to obey me."

Julia smiled and her eyes twinkled.

"What you are now doing is asserting your authority and making me feel that I did the wrong thing when I first talked to you."

"Of course I am," the Duke agreed. "You have to look up to me and admire me, that is what every Chieftain asks from the people he rules over."

Julia chuckled.

At the same time she was thinking that, if she did not give away all the money that she had so generously promised, she would be able to put off going home for far longer than she had originally envisaged.

She had already felt that, as her cousin had moved to Edinburgh, it would be expensive to follow her only to find, after all, that she was not as welcome as she had hoped she would be.

'Perhaps there are more of Mama's relatives in this part of the world,' she thought, 'but this is not the moment to make a fuss about them. I must help the Chieftain to get back onto his throne and then perhaps there will be somewhere else I can go to.'

She was rather vague about it, but at the moment she had no time to think.

The Duke took her up on to the roof of his Castle so that she could have magnificent views of the sea at the front of it and the graceful rolling moors at the back.

"This is about as high as anyone can go in this part of Scotland," the Duke said. "Now you must tell me when you see my land laid out before you, what do you think of the North of Scotland."

"It is just as beautiful as I had expected it to be," Julia answered. "But a little flatter. I expected high mountains and for the moment I cannot see them."

"I shall have to take you to the West coast," the Duke told her. "There you will see plenty of high mountains as well as having a splendid view of the sea."

Julia grinned.

"The sea is always the sea. I cannot tell you how much I enjoyed my journey North in the yacht my kind friend loaned me."

"I am anxious to see it closely," the Duke said. "But now we must go below and find out what we must take to the island."

They climbed down from the very top of his Castle to the very bottom.

It was there that the Duke had his gun room.

There were not only a great number of guns, but also swords that went back as far as the second and third centuries A.D.

Julia was fascinated by them.

The Duke picked up half-a-dozen swords, which he said would undoubtedly have been considered of great value at the time the Vikings came to Scotland in their long boats.

If the owners of the swords could not use them against the Vikings, then they were determined that they would not steal them.

"Now I will add something to your collection which will please the women," the Duke suggested.

They went from the gun room to a room which the Duke opened with a special key.

Once inside she saw that there were several safes round the walls.

"One of these contains very old silver," the Duke told her, "which I will show you another time. Another contains the jewels of the family and a third very unusual jewellery, which was collected by my ancestors and is doubtless what the people on the island would have treasured had they possessed anything like it."

He then opened the third safe.

Julia knew at once that everything it contained was very old and therefore very valuable.

"It was my great-grandmother," the Duke said, "who collected them. In her day she paid very little for them and I am quite certain that the owners were loath to let them go."

There were bracelets and necklaces.

Some of them were made with precious stones which must have come from abroad.

Others were made with rare stones and a large number were made from onyx and marble.

Someone at the time had obviously dug these up and made them diligently into a necklace for doubtless the woman he loved.

"It is so pretty!" Julia exclaimed. "It is just what the owner would have treasured and been terrified it might have been taken away from her by the Vikings."

"That is why I am sure it is something that people would expect to find in your collection," the Duke said. "There are several different sorts of necklaces here which I feel are right for the period."

They were all made with materials that could be found in the North of Scotland.

But they were all so attractive and so cleverly fashioned that Julia thought that they could have trouble in not having them stolen.

She said so to the Duke, who shrugged his shoulders and smiled at her.

"You have to give those who are coming here especially from the newspapers something to write about," he said. "If they think that you are defrauding them, then they can be very condemning."

"Then please do lend them to the island," Julia then begged him.

"That is just what I intend to do," the Duke answered. "But you have to promise me that you will make my people realise that they must guard it securely by night and day."

"I will make them do that," Julia promised.

"I believe you can make people do anything," the Duke replied. "I cannot understand how anyone has let you run away to Scotland when you must be so valuable to those who we have always thought of as being very strong and powerful, although they failed to conquer us."

"But you must not think of it like that," Julia said. "My mother, who was Scottish, loved the English and I can assure you that everyone in our villages and on our estate really loved her."

She spoke without thinking.

Only as the words fell from her lips, did she realise that the Duke was looking at her curiously.

"Your estate?" he said questioningly. "Where is that? I know England fairly well, having been at Oxford. I may have visited your home."

Julia felt that this was very likely.

Then she said quickly,

"I would love to tell you about it, but I think that now we should go back to the island as soon as possible just in case, as you have already said, the newspapers will be on their way thinking that there is an exciting story to be gleaned and they don't want to miss it."

"You are right," the Duke agreed. "But I hope to bring you back here another day. In point of fact tomorrow if it is possible."

Julia did not answer.

She was thinking that she had been very stupid in saying what she had just said.

If the Duke, who had been at Oxford, talked about her to any of his friends, he might easily inadvertently learn who her father was.

'Whatever happens,' she thought, 'I will not go home. My stepmother will be determined to force me into marriage, although I hope by this time that Hubert will have set off for the East and be away for a very long time.'

They walked back through the flower garden to where the Duke's rowboat was waiting for them.

"I have a great deal more to show you," he said, "unless you are now bored by my Castle."

"I think it is the most beautiful Castle I have ever seen," Julia replied. "I never imagined that anyone in Scotland would have such an amazing collection of pictures, furniture and *objets d'art*."

"You have only seen one half of it and I insist on you viewing the rest," the Duke answered.

They climbed into the Duke's rowboat and the oarsmen rowed them rapidly North towards the island.

As they went along, the Duke pointed out to Julia what he believed would interest her on the shore they were passing by.

There was one place where he told her that there was a statue of his grandfather and another where there had been a battle and the Scottish had defeated the English.

"That must give you great satisfaction!" Julia said. "But thank goodness we are no longer at war."

"No one is more grateful than I am," the Duke replied. "The numbers of visitors coming to Scotland every year tell me that the people on both sides of the border are getting on well together."

When they came within sight of the island, Julia said to him,

"You must come and put in your treasures while I take out those which belong to the Captain. You must impress those who are watching over the hidden treasure how important your contribution is and that you would be very upset if any of it was stolen or went missing during the night."

"I will certainly give them my orders," the Duke said with a smile. "I am quite certain, being Scots, that they will obey me."

"But it's no joke," Julia insisted, "and I should feel very guilty if you lost any of those beautiful necklaces, which every woman who sees them will want to own."

"Perhaps we should put barbed wire round the treasure," the Duke suggested. "But it is an insult to say that the Scots are as bad at thieving as the Vikings were."

"I think if the history books are correct the Vikings were rather more concerned with carrying off the Scottish women than seeking treasures!" Julia remarked.

"There I think you are wrong," he contradicted her. "In fact if my history books are right, they took away a great number of things including sheep and cattle, as well as anything easily portable."

"For once they are paying back some of the damage they did then in helping the people today," Julia said.

"Thanks to you," the Duke added, "and I mean that with all sincerity. I will always be grateful for what you have done for my people and perhaps one day I will find the right words in which to express my gratitude."

"You are making me feel embarrassed," Julia protested. "So I am glad we have arrived at the island."

As she spoke one of the oarsmen then sprang out of the rowboat and held it steady while she and the Duke clambered out onto dry land.

He was carrying all the items they had chosen with the exception of the jewels, which Julia held tightly in a black bag.

As they climbed up to The Castle, several visitors were leaving.

They looked at Julia and the Duke with curiosity.

They hurried past them and went into The Castle to find, to Julia's relief, that there were no other visitors there.

"Have you had many today?" she asked the woman at the door.

"Only ten since you were last here," she replied, "but I am certain we will have more tomorrow."

She was counting with satisfaction the money that was laid out on the table.

"I am sure we shall," Julia replied, "and His Grace has brought some superb additions for the collection from his own Castle."

"I'm glad about that," the woman answered. "I thought one person in particular expected more than she found. But then she was a woman and kept telling everyone that, if she had to run away from the Vikings, the one thing she would hide would be her jewels."

Julia laughed.

"That is women all over! While you know as well as I do that a man would hide a gun or in the past his sword."

She did not wait for the woman to reply.

She was following the Duke, who was already bending over the hole and taking out various weapons that he thought must belong to the Captain.

"You see that these are good," she said, "but not as good as yours."

"Now you are complimenting *me*," he replied, "and it is what I want to hear."

"You heard me praise your Castle, which I thought was absolutely wonderful," Julia reminded him. "In fact, I think it is a truly dream Castle and I don't believe it is real."

The Duke looked at her.

She thought that he was about to say something that she wanted to hear.

Then a voice said,

"I thought I saw you going past and I am afraid that I have brought you bad news."

Julia looked up sharply and saw that it was the Captain speaking.

"Bad news?" she quizzed him.

"Well, it is if you want to stay here," he answered. "I have had a letter from one of my relatives on the other side of Scotland that she is expecting me and has a large party arranged for tomorrow when she thought that I would be with her."

"Oh!" Julia exclaimed. "Is that where you intended to go before I joined you?"

"It is!" he replied. "And, as she is rather important in my family, I must be present at the party that she is giving in my honour."

"Of course you must go," Julia agreed.

"I am so sorry to take you away," he said, "and I can see that His Grace has kindly given me back the weapons I loaned you."

"They are all safe and sound," the Duke answered, "and I can only say how grateful I am to you for doing what I should have been doing if I had been here in time and as you see I can now equal your contributions."

"That is being honest," the Captain laughed. "I can see one or two swords I would love to have myself as well as the jewels which undoubtedly will thrill the women visitors if not the men!"

The Duke laughed.

"We certainly hope so, but I thank you a thousand times for stepping in at the time when things were wanted and I only hope that everything you lent us is all correct and present."

He pointed as he spoke to the pile of weapons that the Duke had beside him.

"They are all there," the Captain said reassuringly.

Then turning to Julia he said,

"I am sorry to take you away, but you will realise, if no one else does, that families always come first."

"Of course they do," Julia agreed, "and I will come with you straight away."

"And I have a much better idea," the Duke intervened suddenly. "If you will leave this lovely lady with me, I will look after her and she will be waiting at my Castle, which is a little way South of here, when you return."

The Captain looked somewhat surprised at this sudden invitation from the Duke.

Then he glanced at Julia with a question in his eyes.

She drew in her breath.

Then she said,

"Thank you very much, I would certainly love to stay at your Castle. It is the most beautiful one I have ever seen and I am sure that when the Captain does return, he will think so as well."

"Then that is all settled," the Duke replied with a broad smile that lit up his handsome face.

He then started to put some of the jewellery into the hole followed by his fine collection of antique swords.

"You have arranged them splendidly," Julia said. "Now we must help the Captain carry his spoils back to the yacht. I will be as quick as I possibly can in packing up my clothes, as I cannot stay at the Duke's Castle without them."

"Of course not," the Captain agreed. "You have plenty of time. If I am late in arriving on the other side of Scotland, the party is not until tomorrow evening."

"But, of course, as it is given for you, you must be there in plenty of time," Julia said.

She then picked up some of the Captain's weapons and walked with them towards the door.

The woman who was in charge was talking to another woman, who was standing a little lower down.

To Julia's relief she was obviously not that interested in what she was carrying and merely said,

"Goodbye, miss, I expects we'll be seein' you tomorrow and that's sure to be a busy day."

"I will be here," Julia promised.

She hurried away hoping that she had not noticed the weapons she was carrying under her arm.

The Captain's boat was moored next to the Duke's by the shore.

Julia got into it and, knowing that the Duke would come for her at the yacht, she asked the oarsman to row her to *The Mermaid* immediately.

"What about the Captain?" he asked her.

"He is with a friend whose yacht is next to ours," Julia told him. "He is picking me up as he is moving tonight round to the other side of Scotland."

"I sensed somethin' was in the air," the man answered rather sharply.

He was rowing extremely well and Julia arrived at the yacht before there was any sign of the Captain and the Duke coming from The Castle.

This gave her plenty of time to pack her clothes into her cases.

It was fortunate, she reflected, that they had not been taken out of her cabin and were standing beside the wardrobe.

She put everything into her cases as she was not sure how long she would be staying at the Duke's Castle.

She hoped, if the Duke was entertaining in any way, that her clothes would be smart enough.

Then she told herself firmly that she was worrying about her appearance unnecessarily.

If the Duke had just returned from abroad, he would not want to hold large parties so soon.

Therefore, she had everything that was necessary.

After all if he did have a party, there were several of her mother's pretty dresses in with her own.

She had only just completed packing everything that she possessed when there was a knock on the door.

"Come in," she called out.

The Captain put his head round the door.

"I am so sorry to give you all this trouble," he said, "but you will enjoy staying at the Duke's Castle, from what I hear, and I will return as quickly as I can."

"Don't worry," Julia replied. "We have everything in hand now and the Duke is supplying them with food in really large quantities so the only thing they will want is new clothes to fit them!"

The Captain laughed.

"That is true enough, but I thought that everything was hanging on them and that showed how thin they had become without sufficient food."

"Well, all their troubles are at an end," Julia said. "I am only glad that I was here to see that these people will be very happy in the future."

"They will never ever forget how kind you have been to them," the Captain told her.

He bent down as he spoke and picked up the cases that she had just closed and took them towards the door.

"Now don't you worry," he said, "if I don't turn up for a week or two. The Duke says it will be a real pleasure for him to have you to stay with him. There will be a lot to see as well as keeping the people at The Castle hard at it."

He paused before he added,

"If you ask me they will always bless the day you turned up like an angel from Heaven to make them come alive again and be happy."

Julia smiled.

"I only hope that is true. But no one, but no one should suffer as they have suffered!"

"Forget it!" the Captain replied firmly. "You will be making yourself ill fussing over those people. Although, as you say they are part of your Clan, everyone has their ups and downs in life and you have pushed them up when they least expected it."

He went out of the door before Julia could think of an answer.

She sat down at her dressing table to make certain that her hair was looking tidy and her dress had not been marked by the weapons she had carried.

Everything looked spick and span.

She thought that, if the Duke was waiting for her and the Captain was ready to set off on his journey to his relatives, she must hurry.

She ran up the stairs and had crossed the deck just as her luggage was placed in the Duke's rowboat.

The Captain and the Duke were talking together.

As she reached them, the Captain said,

"His Grace has told me not to hurry for he has a great deal to show you in this part of the country and it will take me quite some time to reach Fort William, which is near where my relative lives."

"I will not outstay my welcome," Julia replied. "I also hope that you have a lovely holiday which you most certainly deserve."

"You have been the most delightful passenger I have ever had on my ship," the Captain told her.

Julia smiled at him.

Then, having said 'goodbye' to the Captain, the Duke helped her down into his rowboat.

It was as they were passing slowly towards his Castle that Julia said,

"I feel that I am walking in a dream. I never thought I would ever visit anything as beautiful as your Castle, let alone stay in it."

"Well, I am very delighted to welcome you," the Duke replied. "As you can imagine, I would have found it very lonely if you had declined to come as my guest, because my aunt is unable to leave her room and, as I returned so unexpectedly, very few people are aware that I am here."

"I expect when they realise it they will all come flocking to you," Julia said. "What you will find difficult after so many years away is remembering their names and what relationship they are to you!"

The Duke laughed.

"That is true enough. I have a large number of relatives who live in Edinburgh, but I have not seen them since I was at school."

Julia found herself hoping they would not be aware that he had now returned to his Castle.

And that for a short time at any rate the Duke, as he had said, could show her the beauty of the MacCarn country which she already found fascinating.

Her mother had talked to her about Scotland.

But somehow it had always seemed so far away and so different from anything that she knew or was familiar with.

But now it had a fascination all of its own because it was part of her.

At the same time something different from anything that she had known previously in her life.

When they arrived at the Duke's Castle, a footman was sent to bring her luggage out of the rowboat.

She and the Duke then walked slowly into the flower garden.

"I never imagined that roses would flourish so well in Scotland," Julia commented.

"They love this country as much as they love England," he replied. "Everyone thinks that it is always cold here, always snowy and blowing like a hurricane!"

He smiled as he went on,

"But as you can see our roses are really beautiful and I am proud to say that they are as good, indeed if not better, than anything you could find in any other country in the world."

Julia thought that The Castle itself was better laid out than any building she had ever seen in England.

But she thought that it would be a mistake to be too over-enthusiastic.

*

When they had sat down to dinner, the Duke's personal piper welcomed her as he paraded round the table playing his pipes.

He was rewarded by a special drink of whisky which the Duke gave him in a gold cup.

The food they were served by a butler and two footmen was delicious.

The Duke explained to Julia that the chef had been at The Castle for over thirty years and was always anxious for him to give large parties at which he could show off his culinary skills.

"I have never had a more delicious meal," Julia said, when they had finished.

They talked of many things, but the Duke also told her a great deal about India, a country that she had always been very interested in.

She was thinking how lucky he was to have been able to travel around the world.

When they went into the drawing room, which had three long windows looking out to sea, the curtains were drawn back and Julia could see that the moon was rising up the sky.

The light from it and the stars, which were coming out one by one, was reflected in the sea itself.

"How could you ever want to go anywhere in the world rather than be here with all this beauty?" she asked.

"That is just what I have been saying to myself," the Duke answered. "But, when I have been here before, one thing in particular has been missing."

"What was that?" Julia asked.

"*You*," he replied.

She thought that she could not have heard him correctly and turned to look at him.

Then he said,

"I thought you would have realised by now that I have been looking for you ever since I grew up, but thought I would never find you."

"Looking for me," Julia said in a voice that was hardly above a whisper.

"You are so lovely," the Duke said, "I fell in love with you the moment I saw you. I knew I had found what every man seeks, the woman of his dreams."

"Can that be – true?" Julia asked him.

The Duke put his arm round her.

"I want you to feel just as I am feeling," he told her, "and there is only one way to make sure of it."

Before she could answer he pulled her closer to him and his lips were on hers.

It was a very gentle kiss at first as if he was afraid of frightening her.

Then she felt as if her whole body was moving towards him.

There was a new feeling in her heart that she had never known before.

His kisses became more demanding until she felt as if he drew her heart from her and made it his.

"I love you, Julia," the Duke murmured. "I love you as I thought it impossible to love anyone. Yet it was almost as if an angel from Heaven reassured me that one day I would find who I was seeking."

Because she was feeling shy, Julia hid her face against his shoulder.

Her heart was beating wildly.

At the same time what she felt was just too wonderful to express in words.

"I love you! I love you!" the Duke repeated, "and, when we are married, we will make sure that every MacCarn in the country is looked after and never, never again will there be a tragedy like you found on the island and in consequence hated me."

Gently he put his hands under her chin and turned her face up to his.

"Tell me that you love me," he said, "because I know I cannot live without you and I need your love more than I have ever wanted anything in the world before."

"I love – you," Julia whispered.

Her voice was hardly audible, but the Duke was able to hear her.

Then his lips were on hers and he was kissing her again and again.

Now more demandingly and more wildly as if he was a conqueror and a victor.

*

It was a long time later that Julia told the Duke who she was.

That was only because she had forgotten that he had no idea of her name or even where she came from except that she was a MacCarn.

"That is enough," he said. "But it will please my family that your father is an Earl. Although I know that they will be far more impressed that your mother was a MacCarn!"

"If you talk like that, you will make Papa jealous," Julia replied. "He is very proud of himself and his long ancestry that goes back many centuries."

"Of course he is," the Duke agreed, "just as I am very proud of mine and, my darling, no one could be more perfect in every way than you. Not only from my point of view because I think you are perfection and nothing will ever change that."

He paused for a brief moment before resuming,

"But my family," he went on, "who consider themselves extremely important, will be delighted to accept your father's daughter and it makes things far better for both of us."

"Of course it does," Julia answered. "If only Mama was alive, she would be so thrilled that I have found you. She was always very proud of being a Scot and thought that they were, without exception – the best people in the whole world."

"That is just what I want you to think of me," the Duke replied. "I want you to love Scotland and to love me too."

She slipped her hand into his.

"But I do," she answered. "It was only that I hated you for that very short time when I saw those poor people – starving to death."

"It is something that should never have happened," the Duke said. "I promise you it will never happen again. Anyway you and I will see to that. We will never be so careless as to go away and not leave someone we can trust in charge."

Julia put her head on his shoulder.

"I love you! I love you!" she murmured. "I feel sure it was my mother in Heaven – who made me run away from my stepmother and who sent me to my own country where I found you."

"I think *I* found you," the Duke said. "It was the last thing I expected at that particular time. The moment I saw you, my darling, I knew that you were the one I had been waiting for and longed for and now we must be married just as quickly as we possibly can."

He paused before he went on,

"At the same time we must invite all the members of the Clan who are available, not only to be at the Kirk but also to come to The Castle afterwards and have the sort of Wedding breakfast you could only find in Scotland."

Julia clasped her hands together.

"That is what I want, that is what I would love," she cried. "I hope all the people will be able to reach us even if they live miles away. Somehow we must make every effort to get them here."

"Leave that to me," the Duke said. "If you are clever in thinking out something new and something that other people can really enjoy, I can do the same."

Julia laughed.

And then the Duke said,

"Oh, my darling Julia, there is only one thing I have to say to you and that is I cannot wait long before we are married. I am so frightened that I might lose you or the Vikings might kidnap you!"

Julia laughed again.

"I am sure if I had been alive when they were here they would not have wanted to carry me away," she answered. "But I want Scotland to want me and I want you and I to do something for the country – that no one has done before."

"We will do everything in our power," he promised, "to make Scotland what it should always be and that is the finest and most enterprising part of the British Isles."

He smiled at her.

"While at the moment," he carried on, "it is sometimes forgotten and neglected as being of no particular importance or relevance."

"We will do it together," Julia agreed. "I want you to be, darling, one of the most famous Scots who has ever trod this – hallowed earth."

"If I live up to what you ask of me, I will be," the Duke replied. "We both love Scotland and we love each other, so we have been blessed and can look forward to a sublime and happy future."

Then he was kissing her again.

Kissing her until she felt that they were both flying up into the sky and touching the moon and the stars.

"I love you, I adore you," the Duke sighed.

Julia could only murmur against his lips,

"I love you, darling. I love you more than I can say in words."

It was then she realised, as if it was being whispered in her ear, that they had found the real love.

The love which her father and mother had found which she thought would never be hers.

It was the love which comes from God, is part of God and she knew that it would be theirs for all of Eternity and even beyond.